Lord of the Senses

Published September 6th 2019 by Team Angelica Publishing,
an imprint of Angelica Entertainments Ltd

Team Angelica Publishing
51 Coningham Road
London W12 8BS
United Kingdom

www.teamangelica.com

A CIP catalogue record for this book is available from the
British Library

ISBN 978-0-9955162-9-8

Cover image by Ahmed Umar

Lord of the Senses

Stories by

Vikram Kolmannskog

To lovers of all kinds!

Acknowledgments

Thanks to John Gordon at Team Angelica for very constructive feedback and editing.

Thanks to Stefan Storm, who always reads, appreciates and precisely comments on my texts.

Thanks also to other friends who have read and given me feedback on the stories, in particular Sheba Remy Kharbanda, Marit Fagerheim Wiik, Viplove Chavan and Daniel Gjerde.

Thanks to queer magazines and other spaces that support queer literature and arts. A special thanks to Udayan Dhar at *Pink Pages India*, Sukhdeep Singh at *Gaylaxy Magazine* and Frederick Nathanael at Pride Art in Oslo.

*

'A Safe Harbour': a previous version was published in *Erotic Review Magazine*, October 2014.

'Ashoka': a previous version was published in *Pink Pages India*, January 2017. The translations of the Dharma edicts are based on those presented in *Ashoka: The Search for India's Lost Emperor* by Charles Allen (Hachette, 2012).

'Engagement': a previous version was published in *Pink Pages India*, December 2012. The poetry recited are by 'Madho Lal' Husayn, translations are based on those presented in *Same-Sex Love in India: Readings from Literature and History* by Ruth Vanita and Saleem Kidwai (Palgrave Macmillian, 2001).

'Growing Up Queer': a previous version in Norwegian was published as 'Bruddstykker av en barndom' in *Folket forteller – Hundre år i Oppegård* (Oppegård Bibliotek/Oppegård Avis, 2015)

'Nanima and Roger Toilet': a previous version in Norwegian was published as 'Nanima' in *Bøygen* 3 & 4, 2014. An English version has been published in *Gaylaxy Magazine*, March 2017.

'The Sacred Heart': a previous version was published as 'Santiago' in *Pink Pages India*, September 2015.

'Surya': a previous version was published in *Gaylaxy Magazine*, December 2015.

'TGV to Geneva': a previous version was published in *Gay Flash Fiction*, June 2015.

Table of Contents

Lord of the Senses

D o you remember the first time you fell in love? A stranger came to your house wearing very simple clothes, smelling of the forest, but your father showed him respect and invited him in. Your eyes met. His were dark but shining. You hid behind your father. 'He is a holy man, princess. Don't be afraid,' your father said. 'He will stay here for the night.'

Do you remember that night? You didn't sleep well. Perhaps you dreamt. Perhaps you dreamt of an earlier life and love. You opened your eyes and saw how bright the moon was. It was an almost burning white in the night sky. It lit up your bed and your body. It made you think of milky sweets. You climbed out of bed and walked down the corridor, as you often did, in search of sweets. But this time, halfway down the corridor, you heard someone singing. His door was half-open. You looked in. Did you hold your breath?

The holy man, wearing only a loincloth, was dancing around his room, his dark arms stretched out, his shining face turned upwards, smiling. The moon showered white light on him, cool on the hot body. There was a scent of joyous sweat and forest night.

'Meera.'

How did it sound, your name in his voice? How did it feel, your name in his mouth, created by his lips and tongue? You had been caught. But his voice and eyes were soft, and so you softened.

'Come in.'

Was he supposed to invite you in like this? Were you supposed to enter? You didn't.

He wrapped a shawl around his sweaty body.

'I want you to meet someone.'

He came towards the door and stretched out a hand. You let him take yours, a small hand in his big. You crossed the threshold. He walked you up to a small table on which were a clay oil lamp, an incense stick – sandalwood perhaps – and a doll-like idol.

'Krishna,' he said. The Dark One.

You looked. He was dark bronze.

'My Lord,' the holy man said.

'But he is so small,' you said.

Were these your first words to the holy man? As you said it you knew you were being disrespectful. He only chuckled. Perhaps he appreciated your honesty and disregard for conventions. You looked up at him, and you both smiled.

'This is bhakti,' he said. 'The Lord can be this small. Small enough for you to pick him up and hold in your hands.' He carefully picked up the boy god and offered him to you. You held out your hands, palms up, creating a bowl or bed, and received him there with great care, his light weight, his smooth surface.

'And he can be as big as a mountain,' the holy man continued. 'Even bigger. Big enough to shake and lift a mountain. Big enough to hold us and lift us. And when he plays the flute, it fills you up. You lose your mind. Krishna plays so beautifully that one day we will all leave our houses, break the rules and sneak out, out into the forest, and dance and sing together under the moon.'

He must have noticed how you looked – curiously, longingly – at Krishna as he lay there in your hands. 'He is yours,' he said.

You looked up at him. He put a hand on your head, caressing you, blessing you.

'Now go back to bed, Meera.'

You had forgotten about the sweets. You went back to your bedroom and placed the boy god on the small table next to your bed. You fell asleep facing him. His pose was so elegant, one foot firmly on the ground, the other crossed over and only lightly touching it. His head slightly tilted to one side. His eyes wide open. In his hands: a flute.

Did you dream about him?

Do you remember waking up at night? You could barely distinguish where his body ended and the surrounding night began, both were so dark. But his eyes were shining like two moons, almost frighteningly white.

Did you trust him from the beginning or did it take some time? When did you start feeling safe, knowing that he was watching over you while you slept? Did you want to stay awake sometimes, like him, with him, and not sleep the night away?

Do you remember his smile? A half-smile. A naughty smile. A knowing smile. You asked him to tell you his secrets and you would tell him yours. You sneaked down the corridor together and stole sweets. You placed some on the table next to the bed.

Did you ask him to play his flute? You hoped he would. And you feared it. If he played the flute, what would happen? Would you leave the house together at night, like the holy man had said? Would you leave the safety and comfort of your house and venture out into the dark and unknown?

Do you remember how you spent time in the gardens picking flowers for him? Small, white jasmines. Golden marigolds. You made a game out of finding the most beautiful flowers you could. You decorated him and yourself.

'Our princess will marry Krishna,' your mother told your father, so attached were you to him. She said it teasingly, but there was also respect and care in her voice and in the expression on her face when she said it.

Do you remember when she died? You became even more attached to Krishna after that.

Years passed and you went from being a girl to becoming a young woman. Your family arranged for your marriage to Rana, one of the most powerful men in Rajasthan.

Do you remember the wedding ceremony? You walked around the ceremonial fire, following Rana, while priests chanted mantras. But the image you had in mind was that of Krishna; the mantra you were repeating in your mind was the name of Krishna. To others it may have looked like you married Rana. But with your mind and in your heart you married Krishna. 'My heart and soul belong to the one who is as dark as the darkest storm clouds,' you said.

You brought the idol of Krishna with you when you moved to your in-laws. You were given a separate chamber there. Sometimes Rana would visit. But often you were left alone with your Krishna.

Was he still a child or had he too grown, the two of you teenagers now? You could spend forever looking at him. You would study each detail of his beautiful body, his large eyes, sweet lips, smooth chest and stomach, his nipples, his navel, the curves of his body, the dhoti in folds over his legs, the naked feet on the ground, one across the other, so gracious, so sensual. Sometimes he caught you looking and he knew what you were thinking and he knew about the tingling you felt. You would blush and cast your eyes down for a moment but soon be looking up at him again.

You couldn't help but dance. It felt like you were a puppet and he was pulling the strings. It felt like he was the air entering you and moving your body, your very own breath, your blood and muscles: that intimate. Sometimes your movements were slow and subtle, other times fast and large. You danced to the sound of your fingers snapping, hands clapping, ankle bells tinkling. You danced like a little girl, clumsily, bursting with joy. You danced like a young woman, seductively, teasing him with deliberate movements, loosening your hair, swaying your hips, slowly removing your clothes, catching his gaze.

Do you remember the richness of his dark colour? It was exciting and attractive. It absorbed, included and encompassed everything, like a womb, like the night. You looked at your arm, your skin almost white. You touched him. He was smooth. Were you stained by him? Did your light merge with his? Sometimes, closing your eyes, you could barely sense where your body ended and his began. You entered him; he entered you. 'He is inside me,' you said, 'instead of sleep.'

But there were also moments of separation and longing. Do you remember? 'My dear lover slipped out,' you said, 'while I was sleeping.'

As soon as you heard about the Krishna temple nearby, you went. You left the house without covering your face. Why would you care? Your only concern was him; there was no room left for shame or fear. And when you first caught a glimpse of him in the temple, you moved and danced like no one was watching, like someone who has longed for her beloved and now finally sees him and eagerly runs towards him. You met others there too, equally in love.

You returned as often as you could to the temple. You sang of love; you danced with everyone. The word spread, and more and more people came to join you. Once even the Mughal emperor Akbar and his chief musician Tansen visited. Did you recognise them in their disguises?

There were also people who criticised and gossiped about you. They said you were a mad woman or a whore. When it became known that Akbar and Tansen had come to see you and you had even danced with Muslims, Rana and your in-laws were furious. They tried to subjugate you. But only Krishna could move you now. 'I have felt the swaying of the elephant's shoulders, and now you want me to climb on a jackass,' you said, rash in your exultation. Eventually they tried to get rid of you. They gave you a poisoned drink. You offered it to Krishna first. And then, as you drank it, the deadly poison became a vitalising potion.

You left your in-laws' house without any possessions, your face uncovered, your hair loose. Did Krishna leave as well? Did he leave with you? Or had he disappeared again and you went looking for him?

'Some praise me, some blame me,' you sang. 'I go the other way.'

Do you remember visiting Vrindavan? Did you imagine how Krishna had spent his youth there, playing and dancing with cow-herders in the forest? Once, when the cow-herders bathed in the Yamuna river, Krishna took all their clothes and hid in a tall kadamba tree. Did you bathe in the Yamuna? Were you naked? Did you notice a stirring of the kadamba trees? Was it him or merely a mischievous monkey?

You danced and sang with others in the sweet-scented shade of those trees. But there was one who didn't want to join you. Rupa Goswami was a respected, spiritual man in Vrindavan. He was celibate and would not meet any women. Do you remember what you told him? 'We are all lovers of Krishna.' After all that dancing and singing in Vrindavan, did you drink a refreshing sweet lassi?

Do you remember visiting Varanasi, that most ancient city on the banks of the Ganga? In that place of priests, what did you do? You fell for one of the lowest in the caste hierarchy, Ravidas, a leather worker and untouchable. You let him teach you what he knew. And you taught him.

Where did you go next?

As you wandered from place to place, your circle expanded to include more and more dancers.

Do you remember walking through dry Saurashtra? What did you feel when you first spotted the many-coloured flag and 255-foot-high spire of the Dwarka temple? As you arrived in Dwarka, the ancient capital of Krishna, you must have noticed how the river joins the ocean there. You went to the large limestone temple. How did it look in the moonlight? Inside the temple you found Krishna, blacker than the night and dressed as a king. There was a scent of joyous sweat and night ocean. Perhaps you remembered the doll-like idol you were given by the holy man so many years earlier: the boy god. You were a child then. Now you were a grown woman – your love songs widely sung – and here was your man and king.

How did it feel? What did you do? What did you say? Did you dance? Did you rest there with him?

You were still in Dwarka when you received a message from Rana. Even he had come around to recognising you. He was asking for your forgiveness and inviting you to come back.

What happened after that? Did you consider going back? Did Krishna stop you? Some people say you merged with him in Dwarka. Was it moksha then, final dissolution, complete union?

'He is inside me,' you said, 'instead of sleep.'

Growing Up Queer

Pappa was whistling, a beautiful tune. He could really whistle. I think Mamma liked it. They kissed. As they climbed the staircase, Pappa pinched Mamma's bum. She brushed his hand away, but laughingly. Their faces were glowing. I think they were happy in this new house, this new place. I also pinched Mamma's bum, and Pappa laughed again, but Mamma said I shouldn't do that.

In the neighbouring house lived a girl who was slightly older than me. She became my first friend here, but it didn't last very long. 'I don't really want to be your friend,' she said. We were sitting behind her house, just the two of us, in the shadow it cast. 'Miss Teacher told us that we should be welcoming to the foreigners, and that's the reason why I have been playing with you.' Foreigners? We had moved from one small town near Oslo to another small town a little closer to Oslo. I got up and left. First I was upset, then I was angry, mostly with this Miss Teacher.

One Sunday Mamma, Pappa and I went out together to explore our new neighbourhood. All the houses were on one side of the street; on the other side was a forest. There was also a small playground. A blonde girl was on the swing; a blond man and a blonde woman stood next to her. They were smiling. Soon the grownups were standing together and talking. The girl was a few months older than me and was also about to start school. Her name was Tina.

Tina and I started spending a lot of time together. I was going to be a writer when I grew up. She was going to be an illustrator. I fantasised aloud about the house where we would live and our life together. She made drawings of it. It would be on the other side of the street, closer to the forest.

One day in our street we saw some women whose hips swayed as they walked. We decided to observe each other. I walked first. Tina said that my hips swayed as well. 'They do not!' I said. Then it was her turn. I told her that her hips swayed just as much, and she also denied it. But it wasn't the same: I was a boy; Tina was a girl. Soon I understood that I also had to be cautious about my laughter: I heard it when I was with other people, a little too high and light. I created another sort of laugh, but sometimes the first one still took me by surprise, coming suddenly from somewhere inside.

There was a girl in our street who was a little retarded. She was a few years older than me and Tina, and we didn't really want to play with her. When we talked about her between ourselves, we sometimes said her name, Anna, with a slow, dull voice and heavy facial expression. Further down the street was a boy who had been adopted from Korea. I saw him looking at his reflection in a window, pulling his eyelids up and down with his fingers until the red inner linings showed. He was lighter-skinned than me, but at least I had okay eyes. And then there were the twins, a boy and a girl, both brunette and good-looking. They even had pretty names, Markus and Elise. Markus had jeans that he had made holes in so you could see small patches of his bare legs. Once he rolled up his shirt and drummed on his tight, sun-tanned belly. It gave me butterflies in my stomach.

We used Mr Olsen's dustbin as a box when we played boksen går. Elise stood by the box and counted with her eyes closed. Tina and I ran and found hiding places close to each other, exchanging smiles. 'Fifty!' Elise yelled and started looking. She spotted Tina. 'Tina on box!' She continued looking. She found Markus as well. 'Markus on box!' I took a chance, got up and ran as fast as I could towards the box. 'Boksen går!' I yelled, and Tina and Markus were free again.

When my cousins visited, they joined in the game. They only spoke English and Gujarati, but they quickly learnt how to say 'boksen går'.

Mamma was Gujarati. Her family lived all over the world. Sometimes we visited them, and sometimes they came here. Ba and Bapuji were my grandmother and grandfather, Mama and Kaka were my uncles, Masi was my aunt. When I talked about them to Tina, she laughed. 'It sounds like one uncle is your mother and the other a cake!' I hadn't thought about it like that, but it did sound kind of silly in Norwegian.

One evening Markus, Elise, Tina and I hid in the bushes around our house and observed my relatives. I had had a fight with Mamma, and now I was making up a story with her as a great tyrant and Big Mama as her loyal servant in the battle against me and Pappa.

Later that week I was invited to dinner at the house of Markus and Elise. It was my first time there. Mamma had warned me that every time I didn't sit straight and eat in the proper manner – or made any other mistake – people would look at me and say it was because of my immigrant mother. While I was trying to eat in the proper manner, the pretty parents asked me whether Mamma was mean to me. 'No,' I said, looking at Markus and Elise. Hadn't they understood that the tyrant and Big Mama story was a pretend game between us?

A few days later Mamma and Pappa asked me what I was telling people about them. They said that I should be careful with such stories and games, that they could be misunderstood. I didn't spend much time with Markus and Elise after that.

Masi, my aunt, was religious and the nicest person I knew. When others were angry and fighting, she would remain calm. When she saw a spider or insect in the house, she picked it up and let it loose outside. 'Animals have the divine in them and can experience pain like us,' she told me. She was vegetarian. I wanted to be vegetarian too, but not just yet; the grilled chicken sandwiches Mamma made were too good.

In the cave-like space underneath my loft bed, I kept the idols that Masi gave me. If not a writer, I would become a prophet of sorts – or perhaps both. Mamma wouldn't let me have incense and fire there, but I had a bell and when I rang it the cave became a holy place and time. Sometimes I invited Tina in too.

Once we were going to spend the night in a tent in Tina's garden. I recounted one of the stories that Masi had told me, about Ravan, a demon king, who kidnapped the innocent Sita and held her captive. It was scary and pleasant at the same time. But then the night became darker and more sinister. I tried to explain that Ram and Hanuman and Krishna and all the others were good and strong and always won in the end. But we decided to move into the house for the rest of the night and sleep there, just in case. Tina's mother asked what had happened, and Tina told her about Ravan and Sita. Her mother said I shouldn't make up stories like that and scare myself and the other children.

At school I made friends with Jon, a boy with big, blue eyes and big, blond curls. He asked me whether I was superstitious. I asked what that meant. He told me it involved believing in a special dimension to the world, and in things you couldn't see so easily; that not everyone was, but he was. I said that I was too. We spent much time fantasising about the journey we would take to India when we were older. We would buy a camper van and drive there together. Soon I spent most of my time with Jon, and less and less with Tina.

One day she told the others in my class about Ravan and Ram and that I believed in all sorts of weird things. Jon wasn't there, and I denied it all. 'Hanuman is like He-Man,' I said. 'They aren't gods and real. It's only a story, stupid!' It didn't work. Others in my class started saying that my family probably even ate monkey brains like in that Indiana Jones film set in India.

The next morning I told Mamma I was ill, and she let me stay home. I watched the Gandhi film that Masi had given me. Overcome with emotion, I cried as Gandhi fought the British. He was my hero. I only wished he hadn't been so thin and bald and worn those strange clothes.

Later that evening I went with Pappa to the grocery store by the train station. I asked if I could have a chocolate. I could. Pappa put all his shopping on the counter first, and then I came up with the chocolate that I had chosen and added it to the pile. The woman at the till looked at Pappa. 'Are you paying togeth-er?' she asked. 'Yes,' he said, and smiled. I looked at her and at him. Couldn't she see that I was his son, that he was my father? But they were white; I wasn't.

I started reading about Red Indians – Native Americans – and I felt a sense of connection to them. I wished for a red-brown tan. I spent more time in the forest on the other side of the street. I tried running with a light foot on the soft paths. On a small hilltop bathed in sunlight there was a large pine tree. I sat on a rock under that tree. There was also a bird there, though I never found out what kind. It sang, and I whistled back.

On the weekends Mamma, Pappa and I would have dinner in front of the TV –homemade pizza, grilled chicken sandwiches, or some other favourite of mine. Mamma would cut up carrots and cucumber and make papadam and dip as a healthy alternative to chocolate and other sweets. Once while watching a romantic comedy on TV in which a man and a woman were kissing, I felt uncomfortable, sensing that something was not quite right with me. I laughed in a haughty way, making fun of the film and the lovers. 'This is just silly,' I said. 'It's not silly that people love each other, is it?' Mamma or Pappa said.

I had Jon's number written down under J in the phone index lying next to the phone, but I never had to check it. He knew mine by heart as well. The phone would ring; I would run. 'It's for me!' Some weekends he slept over at my house or I slept over at his. We would buy lots of sweets and snacks and rent a video. We had started taking karate lessons together, and Jon always wanted to watch Jackie Chan films. I wished I had narrower eyes then.

One day at school he asked me to give a note to a girl. 'Jon asks you.' That's all it said. I gave it to her. She looked at me. 'So? What's your answer?' I asked. The girl said yes, and they began to walk hand in hand in the school yard during breaks, and were boyfriend and girlfriend for a while. But mostly Jon and I were without girlfriends. We spent the summer swimming in the small lake near his house. Almost naked we threw ourselves into the sunlit water.

One evening, when Mamma was away at a conference, Pappa got very drunk. I was watching TV when I heard him talking to someone on the phone upstairs. He was saying bad things about Mamma. Then he yelled my name. I came to the bottom of the staircase. He was on his way down and stopped a few steps above me. 'How can you, such an intelligent boy, believe in all those stupid gods?' I didn't answer. I had spoken with Masi and felt more confident about my faith. I didn't deny the gods this time, but I didn't say anything either. He turned away from me and stomped back up the stairs. I tried to continue watching TV, pretending that nothing had happened, but my stomach hurt and I could hardly eat the chocolate and follow the film.

When we started secondary school there were many new boys and girls, and we were the youngest again. One of the older boys said something to Jon and pushed him. I was scared and didn't do anything. I assumed Jon wouldn't do anything either, and it would pass. But Jon pushed back, and then there was a fight, and Jon used some of the techniques that we had learnt at karate. The other boy and his gang showed Jon a sort of respect after that. I wasn't sure how it fit with Gandhi's teachings, but I realised that this approach could be quite effective as well.

At some point during the Yugoslav wars, two or three new boys joined the school midterm. We didn't become friends, but we said hi, nodded and sometimes smiled at each other. I think it was because we shared something, being darker and different from the white Norwegians.

One day on my way home from school, I saw Carl I. Hagen at the train station. He was the leader of the right-wing Progress Party, and they were getting more popular. I think there was only a small crowd at the station that day. I didn't really notice; I was too tense. I saw Carl I. Hagen, his big, blond hair, and heard him say something about immigrants. I hurried on, hoping no one saw me, a brown boy.

I left a note on my parents' bedside table that evening: 'I hate you. You only thought about yourselves, not about me, falling in love and making me homeless in this world.'

The next day, which was a Saturday, we had breakfast together. Mamma made waffles. We ate them with brunost and strawberry jam or just butter and sugar. I liked waffles – Mamma knew I liked them – but that morning I was tense, thinking about the note and waiting for us to talk about it.

Eventually Pappa said, 'You're Norwegian.' He didn't understand – or he didn't want to.

I turned to Mamma, accusing her of not introducing me more to Indian culture – the Gujarati language, religion, food – the waffle lying there half-eaten on my plate.

'I wanted you to fit in and feel at home in this country, not rootless like me,' she said. 'And your teachers told me that I should only speak Norwegian with you. And religion is something personal and private.' There were no visible signs of Indian heritage in our house. Mamma only had a small shelf for gods, and that was hidden away in her bedroom closet. 'And Norwegians don't understand; they will only make fun of us and our culture.' But she wasn't yelling at me. She was crying.

Soon after that, Mamma and I found out about an Indian Hindu temple in Oslo – the only one – and started going there sometimes. I felt out of place, not knowing how to act, unfamiliar with the rituals, the words, but I recognised Ram, Sita, Hanuman, Krishna and others, and I made some friends. I started introducing myself with my second name, Ram, rather than with my Norwegian first name.

One night at Jon's house he told me about his father's magazines and fetched one of them to show me. We looked at the photos of naked women, and he told me about how he and some other boys from school had met up and jerked off together. Something happened with my penis while he talked. It started filling up, pulsating. I didn't want it to stop, but I changed to a different position to make sure it wouldn't be visible. I told Jon about some new friends of mine, Indian or half Indian like me. 'They live in the city, so you wouldn't know them,' I said. 'We also do stuff like that.' Jon asked about details, and I continued making up a story, my penis pulsating.

I slept on a mattress on the floor next to his bed. Early the next morning I saw Jon lying almost uncovered and naked. He had a boner. It was big, and the pubic hair surrounding it was surprisingly – excitingly – dark, much darker than the blond curls on his head. Did he know that I was watching him? Did he want me to?

I started staying up after Mamma and Pappa went to bed. I sneaked down the staircase to the TV room, closed the door, and turned the TV on at a low volume. Sometimes there would be something to watch on RTL, like German porn with women with insanely large boobs. My gaze kept wandering towards the men. That was when I sensed the pulsation most. Knowing this was a problem, I tried looking more at the boobs.

During the last summer before upper secondary school –

soon to be sixteen years old – I became handsome. I first noticed it through the people around me: I got a different kind of attention. At a party in Oslo Jon and I met some girls. Jon got together with one of them, so I got together with the other. Mercedes' parents were from South America. She told me that when she was little people made fun of her, saying things like, 'So what's your father's name then? BMW?' I liked her. We spent much of the summer at the small lake together with Jon and his girlfriend. We played and threw each other into the lake. But I never got that feeling, the pulsation, with Mercedes, and it wasn't because of her; she was pretty and we tried.

I was admitted to a reputable school in Oslo. Jon was dropping out. Maybe we understood already that summer that our friendship was moving towards an end.

A couple of years later I wrote another note that I put on my parents' bedside table: 'I may end up together with a boy rather than a girl.' The next morning – it too must have been a Saturday – we sat down for breakfast together. Mamma was making chai. 'Maybe it's a phase?' she said. 'No,' I said. 'Your life will be so difficult,' she continued. 'You already have my skin colour. Now this too.' Pappa didn't say much; he just talked briefly about HIV and safe sex. Masi visited us soon after that. She said, 'I love you and am proud of you. To live truthfully and courageously is in accordance with religion.' She talked to Mamma about it.

Fifteen years later our street is still pretty much unchanged: the houses, the playground, the forest. But the people are mostly new. Tina, Anna, Markus, Elise, Olsen and the others are gone. Now our house is also up for sale. Mamma and Pappa are not happy together anymore, and are getting a divorce. I have come to help them pack and divide things between us. In the entrance hall Ganesh sits, welcoming everyone, a blessing for all new beginnings and remover of obstacles. Mamma started to make him and Krishna and other signs of our Indian heritage more visible a few years ago.

Mamma and Pappa start arguing about something, and I wander around the house. I go into their old bedroom. On the bedside table is the phone index and the phone for the old landline that is no longer in use. I turn it to J. I still know Jon's number by heart. Mamma and Pappa continue arguing, and I leave.

Near the train station there is now a shopping mall and complex of flats. There are many more people here than there used to be, including brown and black people, and even some men holding each other's hands. I go into a shop to buy a sandwich. I check that it's vegetarian. There is an old lady at the till. It could be the one who wondered if we were going to pay together that time, Pappa and I.

Between the mall and flats I catch a glimpse of the small lake and Jon's house. Just as I am about to get on the train, I think I hear someone calling me. I turn around, but no, it was someone else. I take the train back to Oslo. I live there now. Soon afterwards I stop responding at all to the Norwegian name I used as a child. Espen.

Nanima and Roger Toilet

Anand and Roger walked quietly past the living room, where Anand's grandmother was sleeping. Nanima, as he called her, was getting old and weak, and his parents had managed to get her a visa to come and stay with them in Norway. The living room had been turned into her bedroom, since it was downstairs and had a toilet nearby.

The young men continued up the staircase, passing Anand's parents' bedroom and the bathroom before reaching their own room. Roger, Anand's boyfriend, was having trouble at home; after hearing about his situation Anand's parents had let him move in. Anand's bedroom was their joint bedroom now.

*

She was back in her childhood, seeing her father standing with head bowed before the landlord as if he was a god. That was how it was: as if they were gods. The landlord hit him with a cane. She was out in the fields and saw it by accident and at a distance. She never told anyone.

Soon after that it was Ram Navami. In the upper-caste village there was a well-known Ram temple. Her community – dirty untouchables, according to the upper-caste villagers – stayed in a separate colony and were not allowed anywhere near the temple. But during the celebration of Ram's birthday the landlord treated them to fruits and sweets.

They had fasted all day. In the evening they gathered under the big peepal tree near their huts. Large baskets and plates were set out, towering with fruits and sweets. Everyone was excited, adults as well as children. There were melons, oranges and grapes. There were barfis and ladoos of all varieties – coconut, cashew, almond – all so milky and sugary and full of ghee. Everyone enjoyed the feast.

Afterwards she climbed up the peepal tree, along with some friends. From there, amidst the heart-shaped leaves, they could see across the fields to the upper-caste village and the Ram temple. The village maidan and the temple, decorated with hundreds of lights, floated like a heavenly island in the darkening evening. Gold and silver jewellery glittered on the upper-caste women. From the peepal tree the children saw groups of people entering and exiting the temple, and they speculated out loud about what could be inside. That is when she had the idea: she would go.

Mingling with pilgrims from another village, she tried to make herself as invisible as possible. Her heart was beating loud and fast. Could others hear it? Just as she was about to enter the temple she heard a 'Hey!' and saw the furious eyes of a priest. He called for some boys who dragged her out onto the maidan, where shabby grass struggled amidst dirt and rubble.

A crowd quickly gathered around her. She begged for mercy. She called for her father, but no one from her community was anywhere close. The upper-caste people started spitting on her, throwing things at her, calling her names. 'Dirty bitch!' 'Ugly crow!' She feared the men would do more. She vomited up the oranges and barfis and ladoos. At some point she passed out.

*

They were lying on their backs, holding hands, only the sound of their breathing in the room.

'Oh my god, this is so weird,' Roger said. 'I just realised we had sex directly above your grandmother. Do you think she realises?'

'I don't think she knows we are boyfriends,' Anand said. 'I doubt that Ma has even told her I'm gay. She probably wouldn't understand.'

Anand kissed Roger on his cheek and turned around to

sleep. Roger looked at the delicate, bronze-coloured skin on the back of Anand's neck, just below his black curls. He inhaled the scent of his skin and hair – coconut milk conditioner, maybe. He kissed him there.

Anand was the first boy Roger had ever kissed. They met at a party last winter. Anand stood out in the otherwise all-white crowd. He was boyishly handsome, with large hazelnut eyes, long lashes, cheek dimples and big black curls. Roger got drunk and settled in next to him on a sofa. He doesn't remember what they first talked about. He remembers the back of his hand touching Anand's thigh. And when Anand leaned forward to get another beer from the table, he placed his arm on the sofa back, so that, when leaning back, Anand's head came to rest in the crook of his arm. It fit perfectly there. He remembers smiling. And he remembers seeing, out of the corner of his eye, Anand smiling. They looked at each other – everyone else, everything else, was a blurry background – and they kissed.

Later that night Roger told Anand about his Romani grandmother. At school they had just learnt about historical minorities in Norway: the Sami, the Romani, the Roma and others. Roger hadn't said anything in class. But drunk on the sofa with Anand, quickly falling in love with him, he did.

His grandmother had died while Roger was young, but he had some vague memories of her. She wore a headscarf, a colourful shawl and a long skirt. She would speak a mix of Norwegian and what must have been Romani with his mother; his mother speaking only Norwegian back. He remembered her patting him on his head, smiling and giving him a fruit bonbon, taking it from a hidden pocket under her skirt. After she passed away his mother kept the colourful shawl but never wore it in public.

While dating Anand and getting to know him better, Roger also started reading up more on Romani culture and history. He read about their possible origins in India hundreds of years ago, their oppression at the hands of the Norwegian state and church: forced sterilisation, removal of children from their parents and assimilation into Norwegian culture. Many survivors were now ashamed of their Romani background and tried to hide it. Roger's father, who was an ethnic Norwegian, tried to beat out of him both his homosexuality and his interest in his Romani background. His mother denied that they had any Romani heritage. She said that his grandmother had merely become a bit demented in her old age. And she said that his relationship with Anand was against the Bible and God. Roger moved out a couple of weeks ago.

He knew that he wanted to be with Anand. Beyond that he didn't know what he was going to do. It was his first summer after finishing upper secondary school. He was excited more than anxious.

*

On one of the walls of her in-laws' house was an image of Ram and Sita. It was the first time she saw them. Next to Ram and Sita hung a photo of Gandhi. It was the first time she saw him as well. He was a small, moustached man wearing only a white, knee-length dhoti and sandals. He reminded her of her own father – except for the moustache, the clothes that looked new or at least clean, and the footwear. These things were banned for members of her community by the upper-caste villagers.

Her husband and in-laws were followers of Gandhi. They told her that Gandhi opposed the practice of untouchability and casteism. Gandhi called them Harijan instead. She wasn't convinced that they were children of Hari or Ram or any Hindu god. But she paid due respect to the images of Gandhi, Ram and Sita.

With encouragement and help from her husband she started reading the newspaper. That was how she first came across a photo of Ambedkar. He looked so smart in his dark suit jacket, white shirt and white dhoti. He was one of them, and he was wearing these beautiful clothes. He said that they should find their own strength and shake off the notion that they were inferior in any way to any community. Ambedkar didn't appeal to upper-caste Hindus for mercy. He didn't identify as Harijan. He said that they should be clear about their situation: they were Dalits, oppressed people, in Hindu society. He called for a revolution and the complete annihilation of caste.

She followed Ambedkar with great interest as he led the drafting of the Constitution, became India's first Law Minister and introduced legislation to strengthen the rights of women.

There was some opposition from her husband and in-laws, but eventually an image of Ambedkar appeared next to Gandhi, Ram and Sita.

In his old age Ambedkar encouraged Dalits to reject a religion that didn't even allow them to enter its temples. He had been born a Hindu, but he would not die one. He converted to Buddhism, because the Buddha taught understanding, compassion and equality. That would be the last gift to his followers. Two months later, on 6th December 1956, he died.

She started exploring Buddhism. She discussed religion with her husband. He remained a Hindu, but eventually an image of the Buddha got put up on the wall next to Ram, Sita, Gandhi and Ambedkar.

When she visited her father, the last visit before he died, she gave him a new white shirt. The old man was dumbstruck and visibly nervous, but he let her help him put the shirt on and button it. Then, over a cup of chai, she shared what she now knew: that everyone is equal; that the landlord and other upper-caste villagers, her father and herself were all caught in a chain of suffering; that oppression was limiting for everyone, including the oppressors themselves; that it was possible to break out; that the path of awakening was open to everyone.

She opened her eyes and looked straight at the golden Buddha on the table next to her bed. The Buddha was sitting erect with dignity and ease. His eyes were half-open, looking both inside and outside. She smiled and exhaled slowly through her mouth. She could hear the outbreath in the night, so light this time of year in Norway.

*

When Roger woke up, Anand and his parents had already left for work. He still had a couple of hours till he had to go to his new, part-time job as a personal trainer at the local gym. He put on some clothes and went downstairs. As he passed the living room, he looked in. Nanima was awake.

'Roger Toilet,' she said with a smile.

He smiled back. He liked his new nickname and that they could share a sense of humour.

'Toilet jana hai?' he asked.

It was one of the few Hindi phrases he had learnt. Sometimes he would help Nanima to the toilet in the hallway.

She shook her head.

'Chai?' he asked.

'Please.'

Before going to work, Anand's mother would make chai and leave it in a thermos for them. Roger poured two cups, and there was a warm scent of cardamom, ginger and cloves.

Nanima gestured that she wanted him to sit on the bed next to where she was lying, and he did. They both blew on the chai to cool it a little. Roger saw that after a short time a thin skin formed. He took a sip, warm and milky, sweet and spicy.

'Roger, I also up rest,' Nanima said.

Did she want to sit up?

'Okay,' he said, and tried to rearrange pillows and lift her up slightly.

'No, no, up rest,' she said.

'Upset?'

She continued talking. He wished he understood more of what she was saying. Then he heard the word 'Dalit'. He remembered that Anand had told him that this was the community his family had belonged to, that historically they had been oppressed in India.

'Oppressed?'

She nodded. Perhaps Anand had told her that his own grandmother had been Romani, that they too had been an oppressed group. Or maybe she did know about Anand and him; that 'our people', as he and Anand sometimes referred to queers, had also been oppressed.

'Ahhh,' Nanima sighed, and Roger came out of his thoughts and looked at her.

She smiled, and then she sighed again.

He had recently heard about breathing meditation. Was that what she was doing?

'Ahhh,' he exhaled in imitation.

She smiled and nodded.

They continued breathing for a while, and Roger became especially aware of the outbreath. It was okay that he didn't understand everything she said. He looked at her. Her skin was dark brown, her hair silver grey. Her eyes were somewhat sunken but had a youthful sparkle. Her lips formed a mild smile. He saw how the breath moved in her body, her colourful shawl rising and sinking. He sensed how the breath moved in his own body.

*

Every morning Roger would come and sit with her for a while. She knew that Anand and he were special friends, and that he had problems with his family; that this was the reason he lived here now. Anand had told her that he wasn't a regular white Norwegian, but you couldn't tell that by looking at him. He looked like a hero in a foreign film: fair skin, blue eyes, blond hair, tall and well-built. He talked with her in English. He had also learnt a few phrases in Hindi. She tried to speak very slowly and simply to him in Hindi, adding the few English words she knew.

When she noticed the oranges that her daughter had placed on the table next to her bed, she thought of a story she wanted to share with him: Siddhartha had been wandering for a long time in the forest. He had tried being an ascetic, hardly eating anything. And he had tried other paths. Now he had found a peepal tree and decided he would sit in meditation there. He sat for weeks and weeks under that tree. Every day village children came with food for him.

One morning they saw that something was different about him: Siddhartha radiated peace and joy like a fresh morning. The children felt peaceful and joyful themselves just from looking at him. It was as if the whole world was new. They called him Buddha, Awakened One. They offered him the coconuts and oranges and other food they had brought. The Buddha asked them to sit with him under the peepal tree and share the oranges.

While they were eating, the Buddha told them how he was aware of the colour of the peel, the fragrance of the fruit, how it felt when peeling it. He told them he was aware while separating off a segment and taking a bite, of the way the thin skin burst against his teeth, and then the taste of its sharp, sweet juice. He was aware of eating the orange while eating it, and that was the path of awakening.

23

Then the Buddha described how, when we are awake, we can see clearly. In the orange we can also see the sun, the light, the clouds, the water, the soil, the trees, the blossoms, everything that has made the orange possible. We can see how nothing has an independent existence, everything is interrelated. This understanding helps us to love and be good people in the world.

Later the peepal tree became known as the bodhi tree, the tree of awakening.

She took an orange and handed it to Roger. The two of them created their own temple, here and now. With awareness they ate the oranges.

*

He watched Nanima, how slowly and gently she peeled and savoured the orange. He also started peeling his, pried a segment free, closed his eyes, took a bite, tasted the fresh juice, chewed, swallowed, and sensed how it moved down his throat and into his stomach. He opened his eyes and saw her smiling. She pointed at the golden Buddha statue on the table. Then she pointed at him and herself.

After a while he got up to have a shower and leave for the gym.

He was on his way out when he noticed that Nanima had a hand on her chest and was making strange noises.

'You okay?'

'Paining,' she said.

He tried phoning Anand, but he didn't pick up. He tried Anand's mother as well without any success. She should be back soon; she was cutting down on work now that Nanima was here. But Roger didn't want to take any risks. He called for an ambulance.

'Everything okay. Hospital now,' he told her.

'I expire,' she said.

'Breathe together,' he said. 'I also breathe. Just one breath at a time. In. Out.'

He sat next to her, breathing in with her, breathing out with her.

'Inhale air and light and imagine the Buddha,' he said, since she seemed to like the Buddha and he didn't know how many more breaths she had.

'You Buddha,' she said.

Was she losing her mind?

'I also Buddha,' she continued.

'Okay.'

*

The ambulance arrived, and the paramedics brought a stretcher into the room.

'What's her name?' one of them asked.

'We just call her Nanima,' Roger said. 'It means grand-mother.'

The paramedic looked at him, white skin, blue eyes, blond hair, but he accepted the name. 'Nanima, you're safe now,' he said.

'Roger?' she said, and looked at Roger.

'Can I come along?' Roger asked.

'Of course,' the paramedic said.

Inside the ambulance Nanima lay looking up through a window.

'You okay?' he asked.

'Beautiful,' she said, and nodded towards the green tree tops that flew past outside. 'You okay?' she echoed.

He smiled, nodded and held her hand. He too looked out of the window, at the green tree tops flying past.

*

Nanima drifted in and out of consciousness. Roger, Anand and his parents sat by the hospital bed. They spoke very little. Through a large window Roger could see the blue summer sky, a few light clouds drifting across it.

In the evening Anand and Roger went home. They passed the living room, its bed empty.

*

Later that night – or early in the morning – Anand's phone rang. They awoke with a start at the first ring, being in a state of high preparedness and probably no more than half-asleep. It was Anand's mother. Nanima had told her that she wanted to say goodbye to everyone now. They got a taxi and rushed to the hospital.

'She says that she loves us,' Anand told Roger. 'She wants me to tell you too.'

Anand was crying and holding one of her hands. Roger was holding Anand.

Anand's parents sat on the opposite side of the bed. His mother was holding Nanima's other hand. His father was holding his mother. Roger found a beautiful symmetry in this.

Nanima muttered something in a low voice, pulling Anand and his mother close. Then she kissed them both on the forehead.

'You too,' Anand said.

Roger leaned closer to Nanima. She kissed him on the forehead. He started crying, out of sadness and joy, and he kissed her back on her forehead.

Nanima sighed, smiled and closed her eyes.

Sweetie

'You're so sweet,' he says.

We're both lying on our backs on top of the duvet, smelling of sex; of sweat and sperm. I have his sperm and my sperm mixed together on my stomach and chest, pearl white on my brown skin.

I taste it.

*

Last week I had breakfast with my mother. She had put a slab of jaggery gol out on the table. She always has gol in the house; maybe it reminds her of her childhood. I realised that she was getting older and that I didn't know much about gol and her childhood.

'Didn't Bapuji have a sugar cane farm in Kenya where they made gol?' I asked.

She smiled and nodded. 'There was a huge container, the size of this room, where they put the juice and heated and stirred it. The process took a long time,' she explained. 'Sometimes I sneaked out with Bhai late in the evening, and we would dip a sugar cane stick in the juice and eat it. I had to promise not to tell anyone.'

I imagined her being a little girl, sneaking out with Bhai, her older brother, while Bapuji, her father, and everyone else in the house was asleep. I smiled at her, spread some gol on my toast and took a bite.

*

'You will laugh when I tell you this,' he says. 'I didn't know about anal sex until I saw gay porn here. In Somalia we would just place the penis on various parts of each other's body. On the outside.'

He gently touches my neck, an arm, my chest, my stomach, as he tells me this, and I am moved.

'But I really liked to put it inside you,' he adds, smiling.

'I liked that too,' I say, smiling back, my ass slightly sore, a memory of him being inside me.

*

I continued asking my mother about her childhood and youth. Around the time she first got her period, she told me, she became very ill. She had to stay in bed for a long time. Later they found out it was probably thalassemia, an inherited blood disorder that leads to anaemia.

'Did you think you were going to die?' I asked.

'No. But I was very tired and depressed,' she said, 'and Ba started fasting every Monday, saying she would continue till I got better. It's so silly, this superstition.'

'Were you alone a lot then?'

'Yeah. But sometimes Bapuji would sit by my bed, telling me stories, stories from India, about life there and our ancestors.'

*

'My great grandmother was also Indian,' he says.

I have told him about my mother's family, that they originally came from India to East Africa.

'You know, Mogadishu used to be a great city, an important sea port, with different communities living there together,' he continues. 'Many people only remember the violence now, but my mother told me many stories about the city.'

'Did you grow up there?'

'No. We had to leave when I was very little. I grew up on our farm.'

He doesn't mention a father. He had already been killed in the war, perhaps. I don't ask about him. I ask what it was like on their farm, what kind of vegetables and fruits they had, how he and his mother lived there together.

'Then it became unsafe there as well,' he says.

Eventually he fled, came here, to Norway, alone.

*

The night before, I had had problems falling asleep. My thoughts were racing. I felt alone. I felt it in my stomach. I automatically went to the kitchen cupboard, took out a large chocolate bar and ate it while watching Netflix.

My mother would sometimes sit in front of the TV and binge eat sweets. Was it when she felt alone? When my father wasn't there? When she was missing her own father, Bapuji? Or Ba? Or Bhai? Did she enjoy the sweets and memories? The abundance?

At some point – soon after Kenya's liberation, I think – the family lost almost everything, including the sugar cane farm, and emigrated to England. Bhai died young. My mother came to Norway on a holiday, met my father and stayed.

I got up and fetched a second chocolate bar. And a third. I felt full, and eventually I fell asleep.

After coffee the next morning I sat down on the toilet. It felt good as I emptied myself. It was just the right consistency, not too hard, not too soft, not too big, not too little. I got up from the toilet seat. It looked nice there, my shit, chocolate-coloured in the shining white toilet. I flushed and washed my hands.

I got a message on Grindr: 'You're so sweet I could eat you.' A lanky black boy; long cock; delicate nose and mouth; Somali, I thought to myself. I invited him over to my flat.

*

'It's a nice room,' he says.

We are in my bedroom. It is small, simple. The walls are eggshell-coloured. A white cupboard runs along one wall. A big bed with a dark blue duvet and matching pillows takes up most of the floor-space. We are lying on our backs on top of the duvet, floating effortlessly on a mattress ocean. At the head of the bed there is a window. The autumn sun shines in, and a warm gold spreads across his long body and across my own, the remains of our sperm drying there.

'You weren't sure at first? About the room?' I ask, teasing him a little.

'Sweetie, at first all I could see was you and your body,' he says in a sincere tone.

I laugh a little. 'It's nice to just lie here together, resting for a while,' I say.

'Yeah,' he says.

I roll off the duvet, cover us with it and reach up and open the window slightly. The room fills with fresh air, a whiff of pine, rotting fruits and leaves.

Engagement

ANGLE ON: COMPUTER SCREEN

On Shaadi.com, 'The No.1 Matchmaking, Matrimony & Matrimonial Site', is a photo of ADI, a man in his early 20s. The accompanying profile lists his age, height, religion, etc.

O.S. Distant sounds typical of a North-Indian small town can be heard – honking, hawkers announcing their goods – and a Bollywood song – perhaps 'Rang Barse Bheege Chunarwali' since Holi is upcoming. A vague reflection of Adi's actual face appears on the computer screen.

> ADI *(Calling through)*
> Ma, you're lying!

INT. LIVING ROOM – EVENING

Red evening sun shines in through a window. Adi is sitting at a table in front of a laptop. MA enters with a plate of fresh gujiya.

> MA
> What are you saying about your own mother! Have you no shame!

Adi gets up and puts an arm around Ma.

ADI

Six feet, Ma?

He stands on tiptoe, smiling.

MA

Yes, beta. Just continue with the yoga exercises and you'll get there.

ADI

I'm not very 'wheatish' either. How about brown like Cadbury chocolate? Who wants wheat?

Ma playfully pinches Adi's cheeks.

MA

In the profile photo you have a wheatish complexion. You just have to stay out of the sun. Don't be so difficult. Amir's mother found him a bride on shaadi.com in one two three. He is not six feet and wheatish either. I don't even know if he likes, well, you know.

ADI

What?

MA

You know what they say about him.
(Silence)
I know you're close friends, and his mother is like a sister to me. But Muslim boys and men are a little different from us, you know.

ADI

I'm going out for a little while.

MA

Out now? You just got here. It's the eve of Holi. Everyone is getting ready for the bonfire.

ADI

I'll be back soon.

MA

Where are you going? People –

ADI

People people people! People here will always talk.

MA

What are they saying? Tell me.

Ma sits down at the table. She seems on the brink of crying. Adi hesitates for a moment, then reluctantly places a hand on her shoulder.

ADI

I just mean that people say all kinds of things about everyone in this town.

MA

They'll see. Soon you'll be well married. Then you can live here and take care of your old mother.

Adi removes his hand.

ADI

You're 40 years, Ma. You're not old. And I'm going to stay in Delhi after I finish my studies there. I can't believe you made that profile on shaadi.com. Did you think I'd be happily surprised? I won't accept this.

MA

I thought this was something we could do together, Adi. Change the profile as you want. Change feet and wheat.
(Silence)
Just delete the whole thing, then! Don't worry about me! I can die here alone! You just stay in Delhi!

ADI
I'm going out now. I'll see you later.

Adi exits. Ma sits at the table and comforts herself by eating gujiya.

EXT. RIVERSIDE – DUSK

Adi is lying with his head on another man's lap, looking up at him. AMIR, the other man, is also in his 20s. Above them is a palash in full bloom. Chirping can be heard from sparrows, mynahs and other birds in the tree. Some red flowers fall on the young men. Adi wets a finger on his tongue, touches it to the soil, and draws a line on Amir's forehead.

AMIR
'So Madho, too, was playing Holi on Basant, handsome and graceful, winsome and coy.'

ADI
Vah! Vah! You and your sufis! Is that 'Madho Lal' Husayn you're quoting?

Amir nods, wets a finger on his tongue, takes some soil on it and draws a line on Adi's forehead. He continues down his cheeks and carefully circles his lips.

AMIR
'Hussayn, in his longing, took on a lively air. His feet suddenly nimble, his steps answered Madho's dance. Madho himself became Hussayn's game of Basant.'

Adi smiles and closes his eyes. They remain in silence for a while. It darkens quickly. Amir shakes Adi lightly.

AMIR
Adi. Adi.

ADI
(Opening his eyes)
What? What's wrong?

AMIR
You were sleeping.

ADI
And why not let me sleep a little, idiot?

AMIR
I was suddenly afraid. I felt so alone.

Adi stands up and looks across the river and towards the horizon. A full moon is rising.

ADI
I was dreaming.

AMIR
What did you dream?

ADI
I don't know.
(Silence)
I should call Ma.

Adi takes his phone out, finds the number and calls.

ADI
Hi, Ma. I know I've only just arrived, and I know that you only meant well. I'll be back soon, and we can go to the bonfire together. Okay?
(Silence)
Yes, sorry.
(Silence, looks at Amir and rolls his eyes)
Yes, I have no shame.
(Caresses Amir's hair)
Right now? Right now I'm by the river.
(Pulls his hand away from Amir)

ADI (*cont.*)
(*Going closer to the river*)
Yes, I'm with Amir.
(*Silence*)
Ma. I'll see you later.

Adi hangs up. Amir walks over to him. Adi stands with his back to him.

AMIR
Something wrong?
(*Silence*)
Adi-jaan, tell me.

Amir places a hand on Adi's shoulder. Adi brushes it away and turns around so they stand face to face.

ADI
When were you thinking of telling me?

AMIR
About the girl? I thought you'd be happy.

ADI
(*Forced smile*)
Of course. Congratulations, Amir!

AMIR
We've made a deal. She knows about you. And she is also in love with someone else.

ADI
Problem solved then?

AMIR
People don't care too much as long as you're married. Why aren't you happy, Adi? We can continue as before.

Adi turns away and sits down, facing the river. Amir shakes his head, goes over to the tree and breaks off a thin branch. Some of the birds fly away. Adi gets up and turns towards him.

ADI

I don't want to be your 'someone else'.

AMIR

So how the hell were you thinking of doing this, Adi?

ADI

You could have come to Delhi. We could have lived there. The two of us.

Amir approaches Adi.

AMIR

'We could have lived there. The two of us.' Delhi is still India, Adi.

ADI

And the Supreme Court of India has just decriminalised homosexuality, Amir.

Amir takes hold of Adi's shoulder.

AMIR

Even if the law changes, it doesn't mean that people will.

Adi tears himself loose. They struggle with each other, and Adi falls in the river with a splash.

EXT. UNDERWATER – CONTINUOUS

Black. The creaking sounds of a DOLPHIN. Moonbeams begin to penetrate the water, and a faint image appears of the dolphin and Adi, hovering, facing each other.

The moonlight brightens. The dolphin song starts to sound more like a flute tune. The dolphin itself transforms in the light. In its place we start to see KRISHNA. Krishna's skin is dark blue like the water. His bare chest is adorned with a flower garland. His golden dhoti is shining and flowing, almost indiscernible from the intense light in the water.

Krishna approaches Adi, places his mouth on his, maybe giving air, maybe a kiss. Adi exhales and shiny bubbles form in the dark blue water.

Dancing FIGURES appear out of the bubbles. Young, old, women, men, hijras, Adi's mother, all appear and disappear in a circular dance.

Amir appears, catches hold of Adi, and swims with him towards the surface.

EXT. RIVERSIDE – CONTINUOUS

Amir and Adi break the surface and gasp for air. Palash flowers float around them on the moonlit water. They flounder towards the riverbank.

EXT. MAIDAN – NIGHT

In a spacious maidan a bonfire blazes, and PEOPLE are gathered around it. At some distance from the fire Amir is standing with AMIR'S MOTHER and AMIR'S LITTLE BROTHER. Adi walks over to them. He nods to Amir's brother and turns to Amir's mother.

ADI

Salaam, Auntie.

AMIR'S MOTHER

Salaam, beta.
(Looks around)
Where is your mother?

ADI

She wasn't feeling well.

AMIR'S MOTHER

Oh?

ADI

It will pass.

HIJRAS come up to them, clapping, singing and dancing in an exaggeratedly feminine and sexual style. Amir's mother quickly hands them some money to get rid of them. The hijras take the money, give them a blessing and leave. Amir's mother turns her attention to Adi.

AMIR'S MOTHER

You've heard that we have a bride for Amir?

ADI

Yes.

AMIR'S MOTHER

We're very happy. I'm sure you'll find someone soon as well.

ADI

I've already found someone.

AMIR'S MOTHER

Oh? Who is the lucky girl? Is it someone in Delhi? Someone you're studying with? Is it through Shaadi.com?

ADI

It's a boy. A very unlucky, Muslim boy.

AMIR'S MOTHER
(Ignoring this)
You must be about to finish university, beta? Your mother misses you so much, you know. It will be

good for her to have you back here and married.

Adi sends Amir a look.

AMIR
Ammi, we have to talk.

AMIR'S MOTHER
No.
(Places her hands on her head)
I don't seem to feel very well either. Maybe it's something in the air. I want to go home.

AMIR
(Turns to Amir's little brother)
Can you take her? I want to stay here with Adi.

AMIR'S LITTLE BROTHER
Okay, Bhaiya.

Amir's mother looks troubled but turns and walks away with Amir's little brother.

There is quite a crowd around the bonfire now. Adi takes Amir's hand. They smile at each other.

They walk around the fire together.

Close-up of the fire.

Tower of Silence

I wake to the sound of birds and look out of the window. The Airbnb flat I have rented in Pali Hill is on the top floor of a posh high-rise, towering above white bungalows and lush green trees. Nearby is the sea. Above everything, the buildings and trees and ocean, high up in the cloudless blue sky, I spot the kites. The big, brown birds are soaring, swooping down and then turning back up. Their quivering screams make my heart soar too, and I remember the Tower of Silence. Ever since I heard about it I have been attracted to the Parsi ritual of serving one's dead body to the birds, a final act of charity.

I take a photo of the view with my phone and send it to Papa and Ma. Ma quickly messages me back. 'So beautiful! I'm glad you're well. Love you, my son.' They want me to follow my dreams and be happy. And this is a dream of mine, to live in Bombay for a while and write. They make it possible by paying for it, and they don't ask for anything back. 'Love you both so much,' I text her.

A small, elderly man in uniform opens the door to the lift for me. As we descend in silence I get an idea for a story, or various stories, of people in a Bombay building like this one, narrated by a lift-wala. We reach the ground floor and I come back out of my thoughts. I look at the lift-wala and feel bad: He is real, and I don't know anything about him. 'Thank you,' I say and exit.

Outside it is warm and humid. Like a womb, I think to myself, and I like the idea of being born or reborn in Bombay, being birthed by Bombay. Along the road is an abundance of trees and flowers, gulmohar, neem, ashoka, almond, mango, jasmine, bougainvillea. A banyan spreads its aerial roots across the paved road, trying to become a whole forest of trees. In the smallest crack in a wall or the pavement something grows. It is so lush I almost laugh. This was all forest once. Perhaps it will be once again. We may think we can destroy everything. But we can't. Not really, or I don't think so. I don't want to think so. It feels good to think that life will somehow always go on, with or without us.

Ahead of me are two schoolboys, uniformed, walking hand in hand. They remind me of Azad and me. When we were in school, we fantasised about moving to Bombay together. He dreamed of Bollywood, of becoming an actor; I could write film scripts. We could go to Marine Drive and watch the sun set over the ocean, hand in hand, Bollywood-style. I wonder where he is now, what he is like, what he does. I search on Facebook while I walk down the road, but I can't find him. Maybe I've got his surname wrong.

I have entered a busier road and stop outside a stationery shop. I go in and buy a notebook – 'name', 'school', 'sub', 'std' on the front cover. Just next door is the café some friends have recommended, The Bagel Shop. I order a coffee and sit down. I text with family and friends back home in Norway and here. I agree to meet up with some of the Bombay-based friends over the next couple of days. One of them mentions that I need to check out the boys in this neighbourhood of Bombay, 'the Bandra boys'. I log on to Grindr, Scruff and other apps, and leave the phone on the table, waiting for the fish to bite.

I open the notebook. The last few pages have quotes by Gandhi, Einstein and Vivekananda – to edify the school children who normally buy these books, I assume. I just need to start writing something, I think to myself. I write about the day so far, what I notice around me here and now, anything that comes to mind, stream of consciousness. A few pages in and half-way through my coffee, I check my phone. The Grindr icon shows 25 responses, a pretty good catch. I alternate between reading the words of Gandhi, Einstein and Vivekananda and looking through the Grindr messages. Maybe I could use the juxtaposition as material for a poem or something.

'How r u, sexy?'

'In a gentle way you can shake the world.'

'What are you looking for here?'

'The best way to find yourself is to lose yourself in the service of others.'

I admire a photo of a full, rounded ass and slightly arched lower back.

'When I admire the wonders of a sunset or the beauty of the moon, my soul expands in the worship of the creator.'

'Top or bottom?'

I hypothesise from cut and uncut cocks, nicknames, language, looks and more, that the Grindr guys are Hindu, Muslim, Parsi, Christian, young, old, of various castes, classes and linguistic regions. Desire brings us together.

'Hi.' He is taller and more muscular than the others, though his skin, fawn and freckled, make him look cute and boyish. I write back and attach some photos, revealing more body, and get a quick response which includes a dick pic – and what a dick! Instantly, in the middle of The Bagel Shop, I'm hard. His cock has been transported from his phone to my phone to my mind, where it is already entering and filling me. And my phone in my hand is like I'm holding his cock. The whole world is cock now. I look around; the other customers and staff seem to be in a different world. I look at my phone again; to them it is only a phone.

We continue texting, exchanging names and getting more personal. I try out his name – Adel – in my mouth; I like it. I write a longer message, ending with a suggestion to meet, 'tomorrow evening, for example.'

There is no reply.

Maybe he got busy at work. I decide to find a gym and go for a workout. I google and find a Gold's Gym nearby.

On my way there a boy runs up to me, stretching out a hand. I gesture no with my head. It wouldn't help him. I have heard about the begging mafias, using children that should be in school. The boy continues to follow me. 'No!' I snap. He gestures with his hand towards his mouth that he wants food, 'khane'. I enter the gym. The boy is out of sight, but not entirely out of mind. I could have just bought him some food. Why was I so aggressive with him? I felt pestered by him. But that isn't it, not really. It's the unjust order of things. My own privileged position, my sense of helplessness, all of this was displaced into aggression towards that boy. I buy myself an expensive gym membership – with my parents' money. I will offer to buy him some food if I see him afterwards. At least I can do that. Lifting, pushing and pulling heavy weights, running until I almost collapse, I feel somewhat better.

Outside again I don't see the boy. But I am hungry myself now. I spot Suzette Crêperie & Café across the street, cross over and order a meal there. While I wait I google Tower of Silence. I read about how the Parsis are no longer eaten. In 2006 Dhun Baria discovered that the body of her mother was still there after nine months. The people who handle the corpses told her that the process could even take years now. Dhun Baria got them to take photos, and spread the photos, sparking a debate in the Parsi community and beyond. Historically vultures would finish off the bodies in no time. But the majority of India's vultures are dead; most likely it's the introduction of certain drugs into livestock that have killed them off. Kites and other scavenger birds still come, but they are smaller and don't eat as much. My food arrives. I look at it and feel sad. We've fucked up nature so much. I continue reading about how the Parsis have now resorted to modern technology. Solar panels quicken the decomposition of the bodies.

I check Grindr again. The dot is green, so Adel is online, but he still hasn't responded. It has been three hours since my last message. Why is he online and not responding? Still searching for what he really wants, perhaps. Can I write him another message? I decide I should wait a little longer and see if he responds. I ask for the bill, pay and leave.

No, I want to write him a message now. I stop just outside the café. I write that I am not sure whether he got my last message – it does happen on Grindr sometimes, I tell myself – and ask if he perhaps wants to meet up tomorrow. He writes back immediately: he does want to meet. We message back and forth, a nice flow again now. He suggests a place; he has a lot of work these days but will try to leave early, 'meet around 7 there?' It must mean that he is eager, surely. I send him a smiley. From the corner of my eye I see something move: a little mouse runs almost across my foot and darts into a hole. It startles me, but then I feel a sense of care and appreciation. I put away my phone and head back to the flat.

The small, elderly man opens the door to the lift. 'Hello,' I say and smile. He smiles back. 'Ho gaya?' he asks. I nod, though I am not sure what I have finished or completed, just the day perhaps.

As I enter the flat and start undressing, I am still thinking about his question and my answer. How was my day? Is it complete? Have I done anything meaningful? I have got a date tomorrow. I doubt that I have written anything good. I doubt that I have been of any service to others. The sunshine softly strokes my face and chest. I move closer to the window. The sun is spectacularly red as it sets over the ocean. I take off my boxers and stand there naked, eyes closed, letting myself be enveloped by the balmy light. I hear the kites, and my heart soars.

I take a long shower, the warm water relaxing my muscles, covering me from top to toe, running down, washing me.

I lie on the bed, write a little bit in the notebook and read some of the inspiring quotes. I text Papa and Ma, telling them how much I appreciate their support, ending with 'love you.' I close my eyes, and memories run across my mind: the boy begging, the mouse, the banyan, the school boys, Azad and me as young boys, Adel, the lift-wala, the kites.

Half-asleep I hear some dramatic music, perhaps the neighbours watching a Bollywood film. I need to take a piss. I get out of bed and make my way down the dim hallway. I notice that the window in the kitchen is open. For a moment I wonder if the birds might come in through that window.

Ravan Leela

The cock is long, thick and dark; the veins so visible I can almost hear the blood pulsating just from looking at the photo on my phone. It makes me doubt my vegetarianism.

'Breakfast, beta,' Ma calls out.

I put the phone away. On my way to the dining room I pass Nanima's room. I see Ma trying to help her up from bed.

'Red!' Nanima says. 'I didn't know my daughter was remarrying.' Ma is wearing a new skirt, some red stripes on it. Nanima has been wearing widow white since Nana passed away.

'Do you want to join us or shall I bring your food in here?' Ma asks her.

'With what crockery?' Nanima shoots back. 'I may be a widow, but I won't eat out of the same crockery as an untouchable. We are Brahmin after all.'

Ma closes her eyes and shakes her head.

As she leaves the room, Nanima mumbles, yet clear enough for us to hear, 'Eh, Ram! This is truly Kali Yuga. I'm glad I'll soon be gone.'

Ma and I sit down in the dining room to have chai and toast.

'I think you look good in that skirt, Ma.'

She responds with a faint smile.

'So what's wrong with Nanima? What was that comment about crockery?'

'We were chatting away happily before my colleagues came over for dinner yesterday, and I told her that our culture editor's family comes from the same village as us. She asked about his family name, and I told her. Then, while watching me set the table, she asked if I wasn't going to use separate crockery and cutlery for him.'

'What?'

'She started telling me how she understands that these are different times, that we're in the city, that they can come here to eat, but shouldn't they at least eat from a different set of crockery and cutlery?'

'Are you serious?'

'I don't know what's happening. This was never an issue when your Nana was alive – you know how opposed he was to untouchability and casteist practices. But I don't want to sit here and talk badly of your Nanima. Let's leave it now.'

She opens a newspaper, closing the conversation. I butter my toast, dip it in the chai and take a bite. I find another newspaper and start reading.

'Beta, do you want to go to Chowpatty tonight?' she asks after a while. 'A special Ram Leela is going to be enacted there.' She shows me the article. 'The troupe includes Muslims even. That's nice, na? Maybe we can take Nanima.'

'If we don't tell her about the Muslims,' I say. 'Sorry. That does sound nice, Ma. But I've already agreed to meet someone tonight. Maybe we can go tomorrow or another day? Dussehra for sure.'

'Achcha. *Meet someone*,' she smiles. '*Someone* a man? Do tell.'

'Ma,' I laugh, 'I'll tell you if there's anything to tell.'

I return to my newspaper and soon get intrigued by an article about Ravan Leela. In contrast to the mainstream Hindu celebration of Ram as the ideal man and king who fought the demon king Ravan, I read that some are now celebrating Ravan as their hero. According to a group in Tamil Nadu, rather than a demon, Ravan was actually a Southern king who opposed the Aryan aggressor Ram. According to some Dalit groups, Ravan was a wise and compassionate Buddhist.

'Oh! I'm late,' Ma says and gets up. 'I have to run.' She kisses me on the head and leaves.

I finish reading the article before I go to my room and check my phone. A new Grindr message from him: 'Good morning, handsome. Still want to meet this evening?'

'Definitely!' I reply. 'I can come to you in Bandra if you want?'

'Great. How about Janata Bar and Restaurant? And then we can go to my place later if we want.'

'Deal.'

A date, not just a hook-up. I smile and look through our chat, from my first 'hi' yesterday through our exchange of pics and more words, the exchange of names, emojis conveying joy and flirtation, even some hearts. I look at his photos. His eyes are like two sunrises in his dark face. His lips are full, made for kissing. I whisper his name out loud, 'Ahaan.' I wonder if he is Hindu or Muslim. I can't tell from the name. He is uncut, so probably not Muslim. Back to the delicious cock again. I close the door to my room.

Janata is crowded as usual: students talking politics and flirting; office-goers complaining about work and their bosses; the regular Bandra uncles who arrive in the afternoon and stay all evening, drinking. Ahaan stands out, sturdy and smart in jeans and a white shirt, sleeves rolled up, looking lost. I walk up to him.

'Ahaan?'

'Sorry,' he says, stretching out his hand. 'I've never been here before; I didn't know it would be this crowded.'

'No problem,' I say, my hand slender inside his big and veiny one. 'We can try upstairs?'

He nods, lets go of my hand – a part of me wishes he hadn't – and follows me up.

The air-conditioned section on the first floor is also crowded, lively and noisy – a TV with Bollywood-songs turned up full volume adds to the din – but a waiter finds us seats at a table with a group of boys and girls. We order beers and peanuts.

'So you haven't been here before?' I ask him, leaning forward so my lips are only inches away from his ear.

'No.'

'Janata is an institution in Bandra, famous for its mixed crowd, cheap alcohol and relaxed atmosphere.'

'I see,' he says. 'I just heard about it from some colleagues yesterday, actually.'

'You mentioned in our chat that you shifted here only recently. You come from London, was it?'

'Yeah. Well, I lived in London for almost ten years. Before that I was in Nagpur. That's where I'm from.'

'And how do you find Bombay so far?'

'Not sure.'

'Careful,' I say with mock seriousness. 'I'm a passionate Bombayite, born and bred.'

'Maybe you'll make me passionate then.'

I look him directly in the eyes and have a greedy gulp of beer.

'And what brings you to Bombay?' I ask.

'I got a position at the Tata Institute of Social Science. I'm a human rights lawyer and lecturer. And what did your profile say? "Beware, I write"?'

'Yeah. Currently I'm trying to write erotica,' I say. 'There's always a chance that I draw on actual events, so I should warn people, right?'

'Maybe there is a story here,' he says, and smiles, his lips full, his eyes intense.

There is a potent pause.

'What are you thinking?' he asks.

'I want to touch you,' I say in a voice so low that he may or may not hear it.

I smile, bite my lips and sense my cock growing under the table. The boys and girls around us are chatting and flirting, oblivious.

'Let's find a quieter place?' Ahaan suggests.

I nod, we finish our beers, he asks for the bill, insists on paying, and we leave.

'You live nearby?' I ask him.

'Near Mehboob Studio,' he says. 'Shall we go there?'

'Yeah.'

I hail a rickshaw, and we climb in. I stroke one of his veiny arms with a finger. He looks at me with uncertain eyes and nods in the direction of the rickshaw-wala.

'No problem,' I say. 'It's Bombay. Relax.'

And he does. He leans back and rests a hand – his big, strong hand – on my thigh.

We drive past trendy restaurants and shops, crowds of

creatives and cosmopolitan people, the roads of the once quiet suburb stretched to their limit. We stop at a block of flats. Inside Ahaan guides me to a combined bedroom living room. I look around the bare-bones bachelor pad: a window with blinds, a large mirror on a wall with a plain chrome frame, a table with a pile of books and a laptop on it, a chair, a pair of dumbbells, a wardrobe and a bed.

'I don't need much,' he says.

'It's nice,' I say.

We're standing next to the bed. We start kissing, his full lips on mine, between mine, my lips between his, his tongue probing this rosy and delicate part of me that his cock will enter before it enters elsewhere. As our hips press together I feel him growing. I sit on the edge of the bed, unzip his trousers, and out it comes. Huge. I bend forward eagerly. His pre-cum has a subtle spicy taste to it, jeera perhaps. I can barely fit half of his cock in my mouth. I suck him for a good while. Then I slide myself further back on the bed. While I lie on my back looking up at him, Ahaan unbuttons his white shirt, revealing his body, muscular, dark brown. His scent is also clearer, reminiscent of soil being turned over or fresh rain in the forest. Once he is completely naked he pulls down my trousers and boxers, licks and sucks my hard cock. He turns me around, spreads my ass cheeks and rims me, his tongue firm and wet against the sensitive skin around or even a little inside my hole. He moves up my back, his weight on top of me, his chest pressing down on my shoulder-blades. He turns my head with a hand and kisses me, the taste of me mingled with him and the beer. While his tongue is in my mouth, I sense his big cock between my buttocks, its head firm against my hole. I want him inside me. Now. Like this. I moan, closing my eyes.

'I want you inside me.'

'Shall I get a condom?'

Does he want to do it without? I want to. But we should be safe, I guess. 'I guess so,' I say.

'I'm on PrEP, so we can do it without,' he says. 'But I want you to feel comfortable.'

'Let's use a condom.'

He picks up his trousers and finds a condom and sachet of lube in one of the pockets. I sit up and watch him. The condom pack is golden. I glimpse something along the lines of 'MAGNUM' and 'XL'. I look at his cock.

'It's so big and beautiful,' I say, 'your cock.'

He smiles. 'I've had guys be so scared they just leave when they see it.'

'I'm a little scared too. But I want it. Just be a bit gentle in the beginning?'

'Of course. I don't want to hurt you,' he says, and even more blood rushes to my cock.

I turn onto my back, he slides on top of me, hooks my knees up to his elbows, and enters me, carefully, and it is painful and pleasurable at the same time. Looking at his face, dark skin, full lips, a little redness in his eyes, I suddenly think of Ravan. Their images merge, powerful and sexy, a little scary, yet caring. I wrap my legs around his lower back, relax and let him all the way in. I stretch both my hands up over my head and near one of his, indicating that I want him to hold me down while fucking me, wanting to submit and be dominated by him, and he does.

A part of me is excited by the idea of a demon king fucking me. Another part is attracted to the counter-narrative of Ravan being a good king, and that I am contributing to this reversal by casting my lover in the role of Ravan and giving myself to him. I am not sure where the one starts and the other ends. Our eyes meet as he pushes all the way into me. I wonder what he sees. For a second I feel guilty about reducing us to these roles. But then I forgive myself: projection and playfulness, a little bit of Leela, is important in life after all, not least in attraction and sex.

Drops of sweat fall from his face onto my lips.

'Sorry. I forgot to put the AC on,' he says.

'I like it,' I say, raise my head and lick the fresh sweat from his dark, shining neck and chest.

He fucks me faster. We moan louder.

'I'm gonna come soon,' he says.

'Come on my stomach, please?'

He pulls out and does.

I touch the cloudy, viscous substance with a finger and taste it too, a subtle taste, slightly salty. He fingers me till I come, and it mixes with his on my stomach. He bends forward and licks it all up, cleaning me.

Later, in the shower, Ahaan takes a bar of soap and moves it attentively under my arms, over my chest, my stomach, my cock, my ass, even slightly between my ass cheeks, near the hole. I like that he washes me. I like the familiar smell of Lux. I take the bar and move it across his body as he did to me, covering him first in white foam, then rinsing it off, revealing his dark skin again.

'Shall we go out and eat something?' he asks as we towel ourselves down.

'Sure. Have you been to Good Luck Café?'

'I don't think so.'

'We have to go, then. As part of your introduction to Bombay. It's an Irani café. And it's nearby, just opposite Mehboob Studio.'

'Let's go.'

At Good Luck Café it's like time has stood still. It is the Bombay of the early Bollywood films. Chequerboard floor; black ceiling fans; rows of wooden benches and multi-colour marble tables, not too crowded now; an old display cabinet with maggi noodles, cereals, candy, and other convenience goods that they sell here. As soon as we enter we dive into the menus, hungry after the passionate sex.

'They have beef kheema even,' Ahaan says, pleasantly surprised.

'It's most likely carabeef,' I say, 'buffalo.'

'Of course,' he says with a disappointed look.

'You like your beef then?' I ask.

'I love it.'

Maybe he is a very secular Hindu, I think to myself.

'Do you eat beef?' he continues.

'No, I'm vegetarian,' I say, but quickly add, 'But I think the beef ban is nothing but communalism and harassment of Muslims and Dalits. I don't support it.'

He nods.

I have a green peas pulao. He has the beef kheema.

'Very good,' he declares as he soaks up the last pieces of minced meat with his pav.

'You should come here for breakfast, for chai and maska bun,' I say.

'I think I will,' he says. 'Thanks for the Bombay induction.'
Again he insists on paying.

'Next time is on me,' I say.

'Okay. Maybe that breakfast one day.'

I smile.

'Can I find you on Facebook?' I ask. 'What's your full name?'

'Ahaan Pawar.'

I get out my phone and search. Pawar. So he is Rajput and Hindu, I guess, just not very orthodox, eating beef and all.

'Found you,' I say. 'I've sent you a friend request.'

'Accepted,' he says, phone in hand.

'So?' Ma asks. 'Nice?'

I nod.

'Tell me more, na.'

'He is from Nagpur, studied in London, only recently shifted to Bombay. He is a human rights lawyer, teaches at TISS, very conscious of social issues,' I say.

'Good,' she says. 'And handsome?'

I nod.

'I'm glad for you, beta.'

'Well, it's still early. But I think I'll see him again.'

She smiles. I wonder if there is sadness in her smile. I am sure that me finding a man would make her happy, but I think she is also afraid of losing the relationship we have now. It has been five years since Papa passed away. Recently I started encouraging her to date, but now with Nanima staying here I don't think that will happen. She is wearing a drab nightgown rather than the pink one she usually wears. Is it to appease Nanima?

'Here,' I say, and give her a red rose I bought on the way back home. 'I almost forgot.'

'What's this?'

'A rose,' I say.

'Thank you, beta,' she says. 'I made some samosas, Nanima's favourites. I saved some for you.'

'I'm really full, but maybe I can have some tomorrow? How is she by the way? I hope she apologised to you.'

'She won't do that. But I know she feels bad. It's difficult for her with all the changes, I think; Nana passing away, her illness, shifting to Bombay.'

'It's difficult for you too, Ma.'

'I told her that we could all go to watch Ram Leela. She got very excited. It's a big event in the village, you know. Remember that year we went for the full ten days?'

I nod. We all went, Ma, Papa, me. Nana was alive; Nanima was well. I must have been around ten. It was a happy time. Tears well up in her eyes.

'I love you, Ma,' I say and hug her.

'Love you, beta. Now go say goodnight to Nanima.'

I enter her bedroom reluctantly. But when I see the old woman in her bed, fragile and lighting up when she sees me, I smile back.

'Jai Siya Ram, Nanima.'

'Jai Siya Ram, beta.'

Back in my room, I scroll down Ahaan's Facebook wall, the sensation of his cock still lingering in my ass. There is a photo of him with a desi dog looking fondly up at him. I press like. There are some posts condemning recent attacks on Muslims and Dalits. I press like. He likes some of my photos and posts too. I take off my shirt, smell it, smell him on it, and bring it to bed with me.

The next morning he messages me on Facebook, and I like that we have moved from Grindr to Facebook.

'Thanks for yesterday, handsome!' he writes.

'Thank you,' I respond. 'Let me know when you want further Bombay lessons.'

'Free this evening? Meet at my place and take it from there?'

'Yes!' I smile and am hard.

I join Ma and Nanima for breakfast. Having finished half a toast, Nanima takes out her japa mala and starts chanting in a low and steady voice, 'Shri Ram, Jai Ram, Jai Jai Ram.'

Ma and I sit with a few newspapers each, reading out loud segments we find interesting to share. *The Indian Express* has an article about the beef ban. I consider reading it out loud, but then I think to myself that it could spur new conflict with Nanima, so I leave it. I look at her and she looks up at me and smiles.

'You're so handsome, beta. Just like Ram,' she says. 'I know these are different times,' she continues. 'You want to find your Sita yourself. I'm praying for that only.'

Ma and I exchange looks. We have discussed it. To tell Nanima that there won't be any Sita would just create unnecessary tension and conflict. She is old; she will soon be gone. Ma reads out loud from an article about Ram Leela.

'Let's go, na?' she says.

'Yeah,' I say. 'Tomorrow, maybe?'

I arrive at his flat and give him *The Indian Express*. 'It has an article about the beef ban,' I say. 'I thought you might find it interesting.'

'Thanks,' he says. 'How nice that you thought of me. I'll read it later. Now I'm hungry for you.'

I want to check that I'm clean in case of anal sex. 'Can I use your bathroom quickly?'

'Of course.'

When I return, he is lying on the bed, looking through the paper. I sit down next to him. He stops on the horoscope pages.

'When is your birthday? What's your star sign?' he asks. 'I don't really believe in this stuff, but it can be a bit fun.'

I tell him. He tells me his. Then he reads something from the horoscope.

'See? We're a perfect match. Marry me.' He takes my hand.

I laugh a little.

'I'll contact a jyotishi to suggest dates then, but better avoid Koushal, na?' I say, thinking that, being a human rights lawyer, he will surely get the reference to the Hindu astrologer who appealed the LGBT-friendly Naz-judgment.

'I'm not Hindu,' he says and sits up, letting go of my hand.

'Okay.'

'My family is Buddhist.'

'Okay.'

So he is probably Dalit. I am not sure how he would take it if I asked him directly, though. But why would it be offensive, unless we agreed with a casteist hierarchy of people?

'I sometimes practice Buddhist meditations like vipassana and metta,' I say. 'I went to a Buddhist retreat with Ma a few years ago. Being aware of what is here and now, appreciating how everything and everyone is interdependent and connected, cultivating compassion for myself and all other beings, these are all aspects that really appeal to me.'

'You see? We're very compatible,' he says. 'Marry me. We could have a Buddhist ceremony.'

I laugh again and wonder what a Buddhist wedding ceremony is like.

'It's sad how Buddhism almost disappeared from India,' I say. 'Thankfully it's been revived a little due to Dr. Ambedkar and the Dalits who followed him embracing it, na?'

I have said it, Dalit.

'Actually I have a Dalit background,' he says.

'Oh. Okay.'

I wonder how he understands my two words, my tone of voice. I want to convey that I really am okay with his Dalit background. We are sitting next to each other on the bed, a few inches apart. I want to get closer to him.

'Do you practice Buddhist meditation?' I ask.

'Not much. Most Ambedkarite Buddhists are more focused on the social and political aspects of the Buddha. Basically I just try to be kind and just. I may eat animals, for example, but I try to be kind to them while they're alive.'

'Yeah. I know enough Hindu hypocrites, people who with their hands pray to Ganesh and Hanuman and will not touch meat, but with their feet kick stray dogs and allow cows to live under awful conditions.'

'Have you read Dr. Ambedkar's text on untouchability, what he says about the origins of vegetarianism in India?' he asks.

'I don't think so.'

'He claims everyone in India used to eat meat, including beef. Dalits usually only had access to cows that were already dead. Brahmins, on the other hand, could stuff themselves with fresh flesh from animal sacrifices. With their many and large sacrifices, a lot of animals even went to waste. When emperor Ashoka embraced Buddhism, he wanted to reduce the unnecessary violence and suffering.' Ahaan stops and looks at me. 'Sorry. You didn't ask for a lecture.'

'I'd love to be a student in your class, lecturer-saab,' I say

57

and smile at him. 'No, but really, please continue.'

'Well, as you know, during Ashoka's rule Buddhism became very popular. Ambedkar's theory is that the Brahmins, to beat the Buddhists, not only gave up animal sacrifices but eventually stopped eating beef altogether, made the cow holy, and many became complete vegetarians. Dalits, however, remained Buddhist for a long period and are beef eaters to this day, the cow being a crucial part of the traditional diet. According to Ambedkar, this partly explains why Brahmins and other caste Hindus have ostracised us.'

He looks at me, takes my hand, interlocks his fingers with mine, and squeezes it.

'I'm still conscious of whom I tell, you know,' he continues. 'My landlord and maid don't know. I don't think either would have accepted me if they knew.'

'That makes me so sad, that it's still like that,' I say and feel tears welling up.

I hope and believe he is at least partly wrong. He is new to Bombay; he may have a different experience here. I have friends who are Dalit and don't hide it; well, I don't really know if they are as open with others as they are with me. I remember the incident with Nanima and the crockery, but brush it off as the insanity of an old woman from a village who is going through too many sudden changes. She is not Bombay. Or...?

'It's like being queer,' he says. 'I don't think most people would have anything to do with me if they knew that either.'

'Hm,' I say. 'You've been out of the country for a while. I'm more optimistic.'

'I hope you're right.'

'How was living in London by the way? Did you feel freer there?'

'I loved it,' he says, pauses, and then continues, 'but nowhere is perfect, of course. I did have some negative experiences there over the years. Racism. Queerphobia. Even casteism.'

'Really?'

'I dated a girl of Indian origin when I first started studying there. I'm bi, I don't know if I've told you that, or if it matters.'

'Oh. No. I guess not.'

'When she realised I had a Dalit background, she broke up with me,' he continues. 'She had just assumed that I was a caste

Hindu, since I was studying in London, was quite well-off, and my surname is also used by Rajputs and other caste Hindus.'

'Horrible,' I say. 'She broke up with you because of that.'

'It was because of her family. She knew they would never accept it. She's not a horrible person.'

I imagine Nanima knowing about us. She would be horrified. But the old woman will never have to know. And Ma, she is progressive. But that we are having sex, that he might become my boyfriend? She would probably not object openly, but in her mind, I don't know.

'We have stayed in touch,' Ahaan continues. 'She is actually one of the first friends I came out to as queer.'

'We're all complex, I guess.'

'Yeah. You can't divide the world into purely good people and purely bad people.'

'True,' I say. 'Recently I took an interesting test. A psychologist friend told me about it. It's called Project Implicit. Have you heard of it?'

He shakes his head no. 'Tell me.'

'You can do online tests of your implicit biases. I have a pretty progressive and accepting family; I've been out to most of my family and friends for years now; and if anyone asked me, I would say I'm a proud gay man. But when I took the test relating to sexuality, the conclusion was still that I had an automatic bias against gay people.'

'Internalised homophobia.'

'Yeah. And that means that the homophobes aren't just some other people we can fight out there. I think the important thing is to become aware of our biases, try not to act automatically and unconsciously on them, but also not judge ourselves or others too harshly for having them. We can bring vipassana and metta meditation into our everyday lives and actions.'

'I like your thinking,' he says, and kisses me on the neck.

'Does your family know that you're queer by the way?'

'No,' he says. 'They're progressive politically and concerned with many social issues. But I don't think they're very queer-friendly. You know how you pick that up through jokes, and things said in passing?'

He squeezes my hand again, and it sounds like a promise when he continues, 'I'll tell them soon, though. Maybe when I go home for Dussehra.'

'So you celebrate Dussehra?'

'We celebrate it as Ashoka Vijayadashmi, the day emperor Ashoka embraced Buddhism, and later Dr. Ambedkar did the same, along with many of his followers, including my grandparents, actually. Do you celebrate?'

'Not much,' I say. 'Well, sometimes we watch a Ram Leela.'

'You should come with me to Nagpur. You'd get along well with my family. You can come as a friend. I'll tell them the truth after Dussehra.'

I smile. He takes my face in his hands and kisses me.

Soon we are having sex. Again an image of Ravan enters my mind. As he thrusts his cock all the way in, I bite into his shoulder, stifling a moan.

'You can bite harder,' he says.

'I'm going to come.'

'Come on me,' he says and turns us around so he is on his back and I am riding him.

I come on his chest and stomach.

Entering the bathroom together – shower and toilet cramped together in the small room – the thought passes through my mind that this used to be their traditional livelihood, emptying and cleaning latrines, scavenging, the removal of waste and carcasses: dirty work. While we shower, I notice some dark spots on his shoulders and arms. Again the word 'dirty' appears in my mind. I recognise it, don't judge myself for it, remember that I don't need to identify with it, and then it leaves me – like a bird leaving a tree, I think to myself.

'What are they?' I ask as I touch the spots.

'Pigmentation. I was born with them.'

We clean each other as we did the last time. While I am washing him, I squeeze his shoulders and neck a little.

'That's so nice,' he says. 'Have you ever tried Thai massage?'

'No.'

'You should. Especially Thai foot massage. It almost gives me an orgasm.'

Does he want me to give him one? I find feet repulsive, even my own feet; to me feet are just dirty. But we are showering after all. And I want to do something for him. I came during sex earlier; he didn't. I move the soap down his chest and stomach, down his thighs and legs. I lift one of his feet, wash it, then the other. It makes me think of charanasparsha. The touching of feet to pay respect has never been expected of me. I think Ma would be outraged and see it as subservient and demeaning. Nanima does it every day before her idol of Ram. I look up at Ahaan. He smiles, and I smile back.

Having finished showering, I take his hand and guide him back to bed.

'Let me try to give you a foot massage,' I say.

'Only if you want to,' he says.

'I do. But I've never done it before, so I'm probably not very good.'

We sit at opposite ends of the bed, naked, legs spread, his feet close to me, my feet close to him. He holds one of my feet. I start massaging one of his with both my hands, paying attention to every little muscle and bone, each toe, the toe ball, the heel, the softer skin between. It doesn't feel demeaning at all.

'This is so good,' he says, and rests his head against the wall behind the bed.

He moans, and I am almost moved to tears, so happy that I can do this and that he expresses how much he enjoys it.

'Will you stay tonight?' he asks with his eyes closed.

'Sure. I'll just message Ma.'

'Then let's go out and eat and drink something. Later we can come back and make love. And we can go for chai and maska bun in the morning.'

'Yes! I'd love that.'

We decide to walk to Janata Bar and Restaurant even if it is a little far. We have time. We walk hand in hand much of the way. We walk along Dr. Ambedkar's Road.

He orders a chicken biryani, a cheese garlic naan and a beer. I order a tomato soup and a beer.

'You're not very hungry?' he asks.

'I had something before I came,' I lie. I don't want to take any risks of being unclean during anal sex later.

Our beer and food arrives. We start to eat.

'Good?' I ask.

'Very,' he says. 'Do you want to try? Oh, you can't have the biryani. Sorry.'

'But I'll try the naan, please,' I say, and he feeds me a piece.

'Try my tomato soup?' I ask, he nods, opens his mouth, and I feed him a spoonful.

On the old TV set they're playing 'Taal Se Taal Mila', and all around us people are getting drunk and talking and flirting across the tables.

When we get back to his flat he kisses me, and I am conscious that he has just eaten chicken but am not too bothered. He pushes against me, his cock growing inside his trousers.

'I want you inside me now,' I say.

'Let me find a condom.' He goes to look in the wardrobe. 'Shit. I've run out of condoms.'

'I think I have one.' I find one in my trousers and give it to him.

He unzips, takes his cock out, tears the pack and tries to put on the condom. He struggles with it for a while.

'Sorry. Too small. I have to order specially,' he says, and it makes me even hungrier for his cock.

'Maybe, if you're on PrEP and it's safe, we can do it without this time,' I say.

'I'd love to. Nothing between us,' he says.

We undress and lie down on the bed. We kiss each other everywhere. I kiss his forehead, his eyes, his nose, his neck, his shoulders, his pigmentation spots, his nipples, and his navel. I kiss his cock, pull back the foreskin and kiss the glans. He kisses mine. He turns me around on my stomach and kisses my hole. He kisses the small of my back and moves all the way up to the nape.

'You should write an erotica about us,' he whispers in my ear.

'I will.'

He turns my head and kisses me on my lips. While his tongue is in my mouth, I sense his cock against my hole, and slowly he enters me from behind.

'You okay?' he asks.

'More than okay.'

I almost come like this, with him taking me from behind. Then I manage to turn around without his cock leaving me. While I am on my back, our eyes meet and Ahaan pushes the full length and breadth of his cock inside me. He stays like this for a moment, filling me completely. It pulsates inside me, his pulse and my pulse, difficult to know which is which.

'We're almost one,' he says. 'Do you feel it?'

'Yeah,' I say, my heart expanding, tears welling up in my eyes.

He bends forward and kisses me. We continue to fuck, to make love, and I hope that one day caste will be annihilated.

'I'm gonna come,' he says.

'Come inside me,' I say.

A Murder of Crows

For a moment it felt like the crows were inside the room with him, the sound was so close, and when the writer looked round, he saw two birds sitting near a wall lamp. But then he realised they were European magpies, and painted, and he remembered he was in a three-star hotel in Bombay. The literary festival he had been invited to attend started later today.

He got up from the bed and went over to the window, which was floor-to-ceiling, naked. He parted the heavy red curtains and looked out, using some of the textile to cover his crotch. Since he hadn't switched on the lights he probably wasn't visible from outside, but he wasn't sure. His room was on the second floor. On the many cables and wires outside, crows perched. That was where the sound had been coming from. On the other side of the street, directly opposite the seven-storey hotel, was a line of basic wall-to-wall houses and shops, mostly two storeys high, reminiscent of a village or small town rather than the city.

The writer's eyes landed on a young man, umber-brown and smooth-skinned, wearing a white banian. The young man was standing near a sabeel, one of those tables with water pots set out for weary travellers as part of Muharram. He filled a cup, and drank deeply. Then he was handed a cutting chai from a chai-wala who had set up a tea stall next to the sabeel. He sipped the glass while looking along the road, or maybe just resting his gaze there, his mind elsewhere.

Suddenly the young man looked up, staring at the writer, or maybe not. Still, the writer felt his heart beat faster and got a hard-on, his cock rising against the red textile, and he covered more of himself. To see and not be seen: it made him think of the viewing galleries from which women observing purdah in the havelis could watch outside events.

An older man in dhoti kurta arrived on a scooter, carrying garlands of marigold and rajnigandha – for puja, probably. He stopped outside Ganesh Store – the owner came out to buy some flowers from him – then moved on to the next Hindu business along the road. Outside Ismail Tailor a bearded man was sitting on a white plastic chair reading a newspaper. A dog lay next to him, eyes half open, probably also savouring the slow pace and peace of the early morning. A woman in a worn nightgown was looking out from a doorway while brushing her teeth, withdrawn but still visible to the writer, watching from his window. A small child, wearing only a pink T-shirt, ran out and looked around. The child was holding onto a package of what the writer imagined were Parle-G biscuits.

A young woman wearing an official-looking vest over a plain sari arrived, dragging a green waste bin behind her. She stopped outside Bagchiis Bengali Restaurant, bent over and used a piece of cardboard to pick up some waste there: the owner or someone else must have gathered it in a pile. The woman brushing her teeth watched her. So did the child. She moved on, stopped outside Ismail Tailor and picked up waste there too. The young man in the white banian looked at her while sipping his chai, adjusted his cock with his free hand, then looked away.

Watching the young man through the gap in the curtain, imagining the young man's cock in his hand, imagining the young man's hand around his own cock, with the fan behind him stroking his bare back and ass, the writer came on the window-glass, milky white. He used the red curtain to wipe it off.

When he looked out again, the young man was no longer there.

And where was the young woman with the green bin? The writer looked in both directions, craning his neck. On his side of the road, next to the hotel, there was a large pile of waste. There she was. She emptied the bin out onto the ground, picked out some plastic bottles and stowed them in a bag she was carrying, and placed some leftover food at the base of an adjacent gulmohar tree. The young woman waited and watched the crows flap down from the wires and cables, gather and eat. Having finished, the crows turned towards her, spread their wings and bent their heads.

The writer got dressed and went down to the hotel restaurant. He had a masala omelette and toast. It was okay. The coffee, however, was terrible, so he decided to go out in search of something better.

Looking up at the façade, he couldn't see the crack in his curtains, and concluded they must be one-way windows. Out on the road, however, he was visible, and he could sense someone looking. He turned and saw the young man in the white banian. The writer smiled at him and the young man looked down, shy maybe, or just not interested in a middle-aged man like him.

The writer made his way down the road. A rickshaw-wala was cleaning the front window of his vehicle with a rag. It somehow moved the writer, the rickshaw-wala in his neat khaki uniform, caring for his vehicle, taking pride in his profession, getting ready for the day. Two young girls, school-uniformed and with two plaits each, walked past him hand in hand. He noticed some official propaganda on a wall: 'Swachh Bharat'. *Clean India*. Then a whiff of incense. He turned and saw the old man with the flower garlands; he had stopped at another shop. The writer bought a garland of marigolds from him. Assuming he wished to do puja, the old man said that there was a temple for Mataji nearby. The writer thanked him and continued down the road, eventually coming to a decent café. He ordered an Americano, double shot, which he enjoyed while alternating between reading an e-book on his phone and scrolling through Grindr.

Eventually he started chatting with a young guy with sloppy spelling – 'veratile' – a decent cock, a smooth ass and boyish charm. He could come to his hotel in an hour or so. The writer considered what to do. The literary festival, the supposed purpose of his visit to Bombay, was starting this afternoon, but he was horny now, and he wasn't doing his own reading till tomorrow anyway. He agreed to meet the 'veratile' guy at his hotel.

The pace and noise of the street had increased. The writer walked back with quick and determined steps, not as attentive to his surroundings as he had been on the way out. Still, he noticed the green waste bin, seemingly abandoned near the entrance to an alley. As he neared it, he heard a woman scream – or was it a cat or a bird? This was followed by a loud cawing, and crows came flying down from everywhere, heading towards the bin and alley. A young man came running out, the same man in white banian the writer had seen earlier, sipping chai, adjusting his cock, looking. Now he was waving his arms in panic as the crows harried him. As though the cawing was a summons, more and more arrived. A murder of crows, the writer thought to himself. As the man fled, the young woman stepped out from the alley. She seemed calm and composed. She merely adjusted her sari and official-looking vest, took up the green bin and continued down the road.

Back in his room the writer opened the curtains fully, and hung the flower garland he had bought around the painting of the two European magpies. Then he went to the bathroom and douched in preparation for the 'veratile' guy.

The writer finished prepping just in time. After a few minutes of small talk, he rimmed and fucked the 'veratile' guy on the bed. Then he took his hand and led him over to the window. 'It's one-way,' he said by way of reassurance, and supported himself with his hands against the glass, inviting the other to fuck him from behind. The 'veratile' guy spat on his fingers and fingered the writer's hole for a while before manoeuvring his cock in.

From outside came the sound of metal against metal, honking, raised voices, the cawing of crows. It was midday. The 'veratile' guy pulled out, announced he was about to come and came with a grunt on the writer's back and ass. Seconds later the writer came on the window for the second time that day.

They said good-bye. The writer showered, dressed and went up to the rooftop café of the hotel. He had chilli cheese toast while reading his e-book and observing a couple flirting – young professionals by the look and sound of them.

Back in his room, the writer returned to the window. His sperm had dried and become solid on the window glass. School children were now buying candy at Ganesh Store. A group of young men and women were eating at Bagchiis Bengali Restaurant. Some people were standing around the tea stall, enjoying chai and gossiping. Others were collecting from or delivering clothes to Ismail Tailor. It was already evening. The Clean-Up truck arrived, and the bin men moved most of the waste from the big heap next to his hotel into the truck.

The next morning the writer lay in bed looking at the painting of the magpies, around which he had hung the flower garland. Then he got up and looked out the window, careless with the curtain now he knew he couldn't be seen.

He saw the chai-wala preparing chai and remembered the taste of cardamom, grated ginger, and the special comfort of milk in the morning. He decided he wanted to go and have a chai there instead of the breakfast and bad coffee on offer in his hotel. He saw the old man arriving with flower garlands. He looked and found the bearded man reading his paper outside Ismail Tailor; the dog was there too. He also saw the young man in the white banian standing near the sabeel again. As the writer watched him he looked up at the sky, his face distressed. Crows were cawing, circling above him, shitting on him. With quick steps he crossed the road, hurrying away from the sabeel, soon passing out of sight. The writer wondered if the crows would forget and forgive him. In any case he could surely have his water and chai elsewhere.

The writer noticed the green bin – it was positioned near Bagchiis Bengali Restaurant – but not the young woman. Then he saw her. She was standing near the sabeel, same sari and official-looking vest on, rinsing her mouth and drinking some water. She received a glass from the chai-wala, and stood for a few minutes exactly where the young man had stood, sipping her morning chai, looking out at the road. Then she returned to the green bin and the waste.

Raja

I must have been in my early teens – a young boy – when I first saw him. Chacha and I were sitting outside, having breakfast before my return to school and the city. Chacha had retired, and now he stayed in his country house most of the year. Our breakfast that morning included apples that we had picked from his garden.

Sensing we were being watched, I turned and noticed some movement in the bushes near the wall that surrounded the property. Then I saw him clearly, standing there, looking at us, looking at me.

He was smaller than me, but probably full-grown. He seemed somewhat cautious, but didn't try to hide or cast his eyes down. He looked straight at me. I found it strange that he was looking at me like this, trespassing like this.

Chacha noticed that I was looking at something, and then he saw him as well and called out to him. 'Eh, Chotu! Aao! Come here and have some food.'

He remained where he was. Then he turned, walked along the wall, ducked down behind some bushes and somehow disappeared out of the garden, probably through a hole. I liked that he did his own thing. Chacha told me that he probably belonged to one of the farms further up the hill; that he sneaked into the garden sometimes but seemed too afraid to come close; that he had told the watchman not to abuse him or chase him away.

A few months later, during the winter break, I returned. It was getting chillier, but Chacha and I could still sit outside and have breakfast, thick shawls and the morning sun warming us.

Again I saw him. Chacha told me he had been coming quite regularly since my last visit. 'Eh, Chotu,' Chacha said. 'Your friend is back. You see?'

He came a little closer. He was small but didn't seem malnourished; and when he moved, approaching us, you could see the muscles working under his skin. There was a muscular elegance to how he held his head and back and entire body – how the body is supposed to move and be if you don't spend most of your day sitting in a chair reading and writing, like most of the people I know do. He stopped near the evergreen oak tree and watched us from there. Chacha put some khichdi in a bowl and, holding it out, went and set it on the ground midway between us and him, but he didn't seem interested. Perhaps he didn't like our kind of food. Perhaps he wasn't here for food at all. He sat for a few minutes under the tree, and then he left as casually as he had arrived.

Once I had finished my breakfast, I took a book and the thick shawl and sat down under the oak tree. I had been there most of the morning when I noticed him standing nearby, watching me. 'Hello,' I said, smiling at him. 'What's your name?' He looked at me. Should I call him Chotu? No. 'I'll call you Raja,' I said. I repeated the name Raja a few times, softly, smiling. He moved closer. I remained sitting on the ground, posing no danger, vulnerable even, with a book in my lap. Eventually he was right next to me. If I had stretched out an arm, I could have touched him. He didn't utter a sound, just sat down next to me under the tree as if we had known each other for a long time.

I returned to my book. From the corner of my eye, I watched him. He was looking around at the life in the garden: a group of small house sparrows hopping on the grass, chirping intensely, a dove perched on one of the bare apple tree branches, cooing, a squirrel running up a tall cedar, the flapping of wings from somewhere, the rustle of dry leaves. Sometimes he looked over at me. After a while he moved closer, so close that the side of his body lightly touched mine. I turned to him and put my arm around his shoulders. I moved my hand down and stroked his bare, muscular back. He looked at me, then at the garden again. I returned to my book. We sat together, our bodies lightly touching, him looking out into the garden, me into my book.

Then he made a sound. I couldn't quite understand it, but it seemed pleading. Was he hungry? I got up to go to the house and get some food. Immediately he got up as well. But instead of waiting or following me to the house, he jumped playfully around me. He seemed to want to lead me away from the house. I turned and followed him, and he was eager now, running, his entire body excited. I smiled. 'Okay, Raja. I'll come with you.' He vanished into the bushes near the wall and squirmed out through a hole there. I went out through the gate. He waited for me on the kutcha road outside. The watchman was half-asleep and didn't notice me leaving. Would it be safe for me to go out like this, alone, here? Well, I wasn't alone. Raja was with me, and I wouldn't go far.

He started up the hill; I followed him. He walked fast, sometimes ran. Just when I thought that he had disappeared, that perhaps he wasn't really interested in exploring with me and had just gone home to whatever farm he belonged to, he came running back to check I was there and okay and still following him. Perhaps he was surprised that I was so slow, or perhaps he enjoyed it, leading the way, stopping every now and then to make sure he hadn't lost me.

I tried keeping up with him, running, pushing myself. There was a bounce and elegance to his running; I tried to let my feet touch and push away from the ground in a similar light way. Muscles working. Blood pumping. Metallic taste in the mouth. And then the view when we got to the top of the hill: open meadows, forests, fruit orchards, fields, snowy mountains in the distance, and a vast blue sky above it all. It felt like I was flying through the landscape. He made some excited sounds, and I laughed as we ran down the other side.

Suddenly loud, aggressive sounds burst out. Some of his kind, but not free: they were guarding a property on the side of the road and I was a stranger to them, a possible intruder. But Raja ran towards them, making louder and more aggressive sounds through the fence, and they backed down. He looked back at me, to check I was okay. I smiled at him, and he continued running, and I ran with him, laughing.

He was taking me into his world. We ran through a coniferous forest of fairy-tale tall trees. Cool. A refreshing, piney scent. We ran along the bank of a gushing river. We ran past orchards of apple trees, bare-branched in winter. I tried to remember where we were running, so I could go back the same way, but I soon understood that he was taking me on a round trip, and that we would end up back at the house. I let go of worry and trusted him to get me home safely.

It was late afternoon by the time we got back. I went into the kitchen, drank some water, and filled a bowl for him. But when I brought it out and offered it to him, he just looked at me. Then he lapped a little, maybe just to please me. I realised that he didn't need me to give him water. He knew this land. He could drink from the river any time he was thirsty.

Chacha called to me to come inside for dinner. Raja was still out in the garden. I told Chacha I had gone for a walk with him. He didn't scold me. After dinner I went to the main door and opened it a crack, to check whether Raja was still there. He was sitting under the oak tree on the shawl I had forgotten there, waiting for me perhaps. But it was getting late and I knew I should stay inside now. I hoped he didn't see me seeing him from the door, and closed it again, carefully.

In the morning my first thought was of him. I hoped that he was still outside waiting for me, and I hoped that he wasn't. If he was, it meant he had become attached to me, and at some point I had to go back to the city. I looked out of the door. He was lying under the oak tree on my shawl. He must have slept there, waiting for me, guarding the house. As soon as he noticed me, he got up and came over. 'Raja,' I said. 'Did you sleep here all night?' His skin felt a little cold. It must have been cold sleeping out in the night. I stroked him, trying to warm as well as caress him. 'My poor Raja, you're cold.'

Chacha and I had breakfast outside again. I had put on a thick jumper; Raja was lying on my shawl under the oak tree.

'I think he slept here the whole night,' I said. 'Is it okay that he has my shawl?'

'Okay, beta.'

'Maybe he's been abandoned,' I continued. 'Maybe we could take him in. Maybe he could come to the city with me. I don't know. Here he has so much freedom. He has all of this. You should have seen him when we went running. But I don't think he has someone who really loves him here. In the city he'd have to stay in the house, only get out a few times a day, and in a very different environment, but we'd be together.'

Chacha smiled and spoke softly. 'Oh, beta. I'm quite sure he belongs to a farm further up the hill. And he's used to this kind of life. It would be cruel to take him away. Perhaps you shouldn't get too involved.'

After breakfast I took my book and sat down next to him under the tree again.

When I noticed our neighbour out in his garden, I went over to the fence between the properties and called to him. Raja followed me. I asked the neighbour if he knew anything about Raja and where he belonged. He pointed to a yellow house along the way, a large mansion. It also belonged to some city people, but I don't think I had ever seen them here. Our neighbour confirmed that they didn't come often, but said they had a caretaker. He told me not to worry. 'Look at him,' he said. 'He's not starving. It's their instinct to survive, killing and eating rats and what not.'

I felt bad that Raja should have to live off rats, and that I ought to be okay with that. But I was also relieved, thinking that there were probably plenty of rats and perhaps they were not that bad to eat. Something was lacking in his life, though. He was peeing now, on some of the herbs that Chacha had planted. I guess he was marking this territory as his. I wanted to be his. He could be mine.

We got into a certain routine over the next few days. I read my book under the oak tree, and he sat next to me. We talked, I caressed him. He took me for runs. At night he slept under the tree on the shawl.

On the final morning before my departure back to the city I hoped I would see him outside, and I hoped I wouldn't. I had to leave him here.

Chacha said that I didn't have to worry, that he would look after him, and I could come and see him as often as I wanted. I think Chacha was growing fond of Raja, and I was glad that he would remain here. I looked out of the main door. He was there, on his shawl under the oak tree. The morning air was cold on my face. He noticed me, raised his head, got up, stretched, yawned and came over to me. I held him. 'Raja. My darling Raja.' I told him that I had to leave now. I said it in a soft voice. I said that he probably had a better life here. I said that Chacha would still be here. I thanked him for everything, for showing me his world, for sharing it, for all the love between us. I said that I would always treasure this time that we had spent together; that I hoped he would too.

Chacha and I had our last breakfast outside. 'Arrey,' he said sharply at some point. 'Don't pee on my herbs.' Raja looked at him and returned to the shawl. Then our driver came. I got up and headed to the car. Raja jumped around me, probably thinking we were going for our run. My heart ached so much I could hardly move. I moved mechanically, without eye contact, without looking at him, got in the car and closed the door. As we drove away he ran after the car along the kutcha road. I heard him. Our speed increased. I don't know how far he followed us. I didn't look back for a long time; and then when I did, he wasn't there.

I have not been back to the country house. Chacha keeps telling me to come. But I can't. Now I only see him when he visits us in the city. He tells me that Raja is fine, that he stops by sometimes, still has his shawl there under the tree, that he stays for a short while, then leaves again.

Surya

I can't sleep. I am thinking about Surya.

*

I went to a party. Some of the guests were complaining about Modi. Others were discussing a recent but distant terrorist attack. Everyone was trying to look sexy and seem intellectual. In English. While drinking Chandon. A lot of Chandon.

At some point I left. It was still early: I blamed it on the jetlag. I found a taxi. The driver unlocked the front passenger-side door, so I could climb into the seat next to him. I tried to open the door behind, so I could have some privacy. But the back door was locked, and he didn't open it, so I got in next to him.

It is uncomfortable to be so close and not speak. I look out through the side window without really seeing what is there. I pick up the scent of tobacco and something sweet and floral inside the car. Maybe he smokes. I hear him singing softly to himself. Maybe he does that when he is by himself, or when he feels lonely – even with passengers here. I don't know the song.

Then he pulls over.

'Ek minit, sir,' he says.

'Okay.'

He gets out of the car and disappears down a dimly-lit, narrow side-street. It is not exactly a basti, I think, but it is certainly not somewhere the people from the party would live. He probably needs to take a piss. He is gone for a couple of minutes. Then he reappears.

'Peshaab?' I ask when he gets back in.

'Nahin, sir.'

He opens his hand: a small lump of hashish, almost black in his palm. I look at him. He is young and handsome, and though his eyes are slightly bloodshot I am sure many men would want to have sex with him. I wonder if he does that. Maybe for the extra money. He asks me something. Do I smoke? Or perhaps whether I want to smoke? I tell him no. Stumbling along in my broken Hindi, I ask him about the hashish. The quality. The price. Small talk. He tells me that this is enough for ten joints. He smokes one every night before he goes to bed. It gives him energy, he tells me. His Hindi is excellent. I ask where he is from.

'UP, sir.'

We are talking now; that is, it is mostly him talking. I pick up words here and there and try to understand from the context and his body language. Perhaps it is good my Hindi is so bad; it levels out the relationship. And no matter how clumsily I say the few things that I do, he doesn't laugh at me. I still wish my Hindi were better, though. I want to understand more of what he is telling me.

He comes from a village, I gather as we drive along. His parents and younger siblings are still there. It's difficult, he tells me, his voice cracking a little. He hasn't been back to see them since he moved here three years ago. I ask him where in the city he stays. He sleeps in the back of the car, he tells me. I glance over at him. He is wearing a clean, white shirt; it is almost shining against his skin. For a moment I wonder if I am invading his privacy, but I keep asking questions. Where does he shower and clean himself and his clothing? And then: what's his dream?

God, why did I do that? It is like some kitschy film thing. But why not? Everyone has dreams. To help his parents and younger siblings, he says. I wonder if he doesn't also want something for himself. No, only helping them, he insists. Suddenly a Neruda line lands in my mind: 'I want to do with you what spring does with the cherry trees.' And then I realise I don't even know his name.

'Aapka naam kya hai?'

'Surya.'

Surya. The sun. He asks for mine.

'Ram.'

'Very good,' he says in English.

I feel more connected to him after the exchange of names. I want to share something more with him: Where I am from. What life is like there.

'Uttar Europe.'

I start talking about how the sun is slowly disappearing there now; how in winter there is hardly any sun, only white snow and dark skies. We live like that for many months, I tell him. It is difficult. But then comes spring and summer.

'Hamesha surya. Twenty-four hours' sun.'

'Achcha,' he says. He smiles. And when Surya smiles, his eyes light up. I am attracted to him. But I don't think it is sexual. I don't know. Somehow he feels more like a brother to me.

'Yahaan left,' I say.

Surya turns left and continues talking. But I have to interrupt again.

'Yahaan right.'

It is coming to an end. What would it have been like if I had smoked a joint with him?

'Yeh mera hotel,' I say.

I am a little embarrassed about the hotel – quite upscale – but he doesn't seem to notice. I look at the meter: 375 rupees. I find a 500-rupees note in my pocket and give it to him.

'Rest is for you.'

'Nahin, bhai.'

No, brother, too much, he tells me. He tries to give it back to me, his hands covering mine. Suddenly I have tears in my eyes. I don't know why. In a way this is so degrading, me giving him this money, forcing it on him. In a way he is so beautiful for refusing to take it. Maybe it is also him calling me brother instead of sir that makes me so sentimental. Maybe it is the Chandon I drank at the party and the jetlag kicking in. Regardless of the reason, I have tears in my eyes now, and Surya takes the money. He asks if I have an Indian number. I don't. And I don't ask for his. He says that maybe we will meet again anyway. I take his hand briefly, and our eyes meet. Then I open the door and get out.

*

It is late now. Surya has probably finished his joint and is sleeping as well as he can on the back seat of the car. I try to think about one of the guys from the party instead. I remember a random guy with a fit body and a nice smile. I imagine us having sex. I come, and finally I fall asleep.

Ashoka

At first glance and touch Ashoka, who would later become known as 'Beloved-of-the-gods', is ugly and unpleasant due to a skin condition. In addition, for some unknown reason, he keeps fainting all the time. Still, through scheming and violence, in 273 BCE he takes the imperial throne and aggressively expands the Mauryan empire. But after neighbouring Kalinga, his most brutal conquest, falls around 262 BCE, he feels deep remorse and decides to rule differently. Now the man with the rough skin, the emperor who has ordered thousands killed by swords, has words carved into the faces of rocks and stone pillars, beautiful edicts scattered across his empire. I catch myself touching my own face, neck, chest and arms for traces of his words.

'What constitutes Dhamma?' Ashoka asks. And he goes on to suggest: 'little evil, much good, kindness, generosity, truthfulness and purity.' I see the wells and hospitals constructed and the trees planted along the roads as the consequence of such a belief, and I love that he does it, as he writes, for the benefit of all living beings. But I think it is when learning the details of his dinner plans that I fall in love. 'Formerly in the kitchen of Beloved-of-the-gods hundreds of thousands of animals were killed every day to make curry. But now, with the writing of this Dhamma edict, only three creatures – two peacocks and a deer – are killed, and the deer not always. And in time not even these three creatures will be killed.'

How wise and patient, this implicit recognition that human change is often slow and imperfect. How irresistibly sweet when also read as a recognition of imperfection in the great emperor himself. I imagine deer being among his favourite dishes, and this statement a disclosure of his own cravings and weaknesses along with his striving to be better. I think I envy the deer a little then. At least this is when I first want to give myself to him, to Ashoka.

'And in time not even these three creatures will be killed.'

What a youthful optimism in the mature man; what a wonderful vision to put our faith in. And meanwhile I want to be held by him, and I want to be there to hold him. I imagine us like this for a moment. Ashoka would no longer have to fear fainting.

Gold's Gym, Bandra West

Facing one of the mirrored walls, four muscular, middle-aged men are lifting heavy dumbbells. As I discreetly watch their reflections, I bite my lip and sense my cock coming alive. I imagine a different time and place, my body intimately intertwined with theirs like pehlwani wrestlers.

They are dressed in sleeveless shirts and sports shorts. Even these almost-bears are waxed and hairless nowadays. While I enjoy the unobstructed view of veins and muscles moving under shiny skin, it makes me nostalgic too: I remember the Suniel Shetty films I watched with my parents as a child. His bad acting didn't bother me; I spent happy hours imagining my head resting on that hairy chest, or letting him lift me up and press me to him tight.

And then there were Dadima's stories about the Pathans – probably hairy-chested too, at least in my fantasies. She said they would come and take children who misbehaved. Even though I later dismissed these stories as unfounded, slightly racist rumours from her own childhood, the little bit of irrational fear that remained made the Pathans more exciting and attractive to me. If Dadima had known that a Pathan would be the first man to fuck me...

As I go over to the cable crossover machine, I steal another glance at the dumbbell-lifting daddies and notice that one of them has chest hair. My hero even has a finely twirled mooch.

He is joking with the taller and darker of the other daddies, who I now realise looks familiar. Has he messaged me on Grindr? Maybe I've just seen him in the gym before. But isn't he looking at me in the mirror now?

Maybe he was just looking because I was looking.

Someone bumps into me from behind. 'Sorry,' she says. A lady who must be in her early forties, short hair, fair, toned body, affluent-looking.

'No problem,' I say.

She follows me – or maybe she was going in that direction anyway – and squeezes me sort of innocently on the shoulder, adding, 'But you got power, na.'

I remember a friend telling me about a woman who he became Facebook-friends with when he was sixteen and she was in her thirties. He called her Didi, and one day, while his parents were at work, he invited her over. She wanted to see their bedroom, and she asked him to sit next to her on their bed, and then she started fondling him, and he liked it and he disliked it at the same time. She liked young boys. I am not that young, but still look young enough for some, I guess. I both like it and dislike it, this lady following behind me, her gaze on me. While yes, I have some power, including bodily strength, I imagine her having much more economic and social capital. It turns me on a little.

I stop at the cable crossover machine. As I pull my arms together in front of me I sense my pecs working, a slight pain as well as a pleasure. I notice the darker daddy coming in my direction. I am still not sure if – and where – I may have seen him before, but he just asks if we can alternate.

'Sure,' I say.

He adds more weights. He is wearing a white stringer tank top. It leaves most of his pecs and upper back bare, along with the latissimus dorsi. Tantalising. I watch his muscles moving under his skin, dark skin shining in the light, and say this sexy Latin word in my mind, 'latissimus dorsi'. At some point his entire right pec is revealed, one string pushed to the middle of his chest. And it looks like his nipple is hard, the AC close by a possible cause of his titillation, though this doesn't preclude others, of course. The music is now a pumping techno. He does a few more reps, nipple in plain sight, then steps aside for me.

While I do a set, making more effort than I was previously to display good form, he ignores me, checks his phone and drinks from his water bottle. Some of the water spills over his almost purple lips, down his chin and onto his chest, mixing with his sweat. I am struggling now; he notices and comes up behind me, close, his arms supporting my arms, his breath touching my neck. I see us in the mirror, flying, him behind me like this. I think we have chatted on Grindr.

'Shabash,' he says when I am done.

'Thanks.' I smile.

'Anytime.'

I go over to the water fountain. Yes, I remember him now: face, body and dick pics. I lean in, push the button. Water shoots out, I move my lips closer, part them slightly and swallow.

Hero with the hairy chest and mooch is doing bench presses, lifting heavy weights, breathing, moaning with the exertion. I go and stand nearby, waiting, watching. There is a whiff of fresh sweat, like that of delicious sex rather than sour stress. He gets up and starts taking the weights off the bar.

'Finished?' I ask.

'All yours, bro,' he says.

I lie back, close my eyes for a second, sense through my thin T-shirt his sweat mixing with my sweat, his smell.

'Spot you?' he asks. He is standing behind me, above me.

Can he see that I am half-hard as I lie exposed on the bench?

'Thanks,' I say.

He moves closer, powerful thighs spread, crotch above my face. I inhale and then exhale as I lift the bar. I am touched when he decides, having noticed I am getting close to my limit, to gently support the bar with two fingertips for my final repetitions.

After finishing two sets I thank him. He turns away to get on with his routine. I remain seated on the bench, ostensibly resting or waiting for a piece of equipment to become free, really just looking. A group of teenage boys arrive talking to each other. They are thin like Indian boys can be. They look around, some sending me looks, then carry on talking to each other. They start doing sit-ups and push-ups. Their thick hair is arranged in the latest styles – wavy spiked, shaved facet. All of them are attractive in a youthful way, like the flesh of fresh fruit, like the creamy white and almost custard-tasting sitaphal. And yet, while delicate and to be handled with care, such boys can have a particular determination, along with a ridiculous amount of stamina. I remember a young lover I had. He would fuck me, come and just continue fucking. And though I would get sore and exhausted, I couldn't say no to his youthful hunger; it turned me on too much, and I didn't want to disappoint him so early on in life.

One of the twinks, a little more toned than the others, is leaning against a machine, resting or, like me, looking at others via the mirror. He wears a loose, sleeveless vest. A silver taweez is tied with a black string around one upper arm. I wonder what he wants to ward off; it certainly draws attention to his delicately defined bicep. The attraction of someone or something telling you both yes and no. He moves to the music, subtle movements that are, I think, unconscious. His waist is small, his ass a bubble, and my hands long to be there, on his waist, on his butt. He looks at himself in the mirror, lifts his shirt up to display the start of a six-pack, wanting to check its progress perhaps. I look at him looking at himself in the mirror. His eyes meet mine; they lock for that extra second. I want to fuck him.

'Excuse me, are you using this?' It is the lady again.

'Sorry. All yours.' I jump up from the bench I have been occupying.

She smiles. I take off some weights for her.

'You can leave that one,' she says. 'I will try with some support.'

I smile at her and leave. I think she wanted me to offer to help her. She calls out to one of the trainers, who comes over instead.

The darker daddy is doing leg raises now, hanging from the pull-up bar. When he drops down he adjusts his shorts, adjusting his cock too, kind of casually, but looking my way while doing it, not directly at me but in my general direction. I walk past him, close, watching him watch me out of the corner of my eye.

I go and sit near the taweez twink. He is busy making his bubble butt even more bubblicious by doing leg curls. He is voluntarily strapped to the machine, a hint of bondage as he lies face down, grabbing the side handles, ass up in the air, not knowing who is behind him at any given moment. Now it's me.

My crotch stirs.

As he finishes a set, I move in and ask if we can alternate. He smiles and gestures a yes with his head. I wonder if he generally smiles and accommodates. I lie down, my cock where his was just seconds ago, our bodies in touch vicariously via benches and bars. One of his twink friends comes up to him. I hear them talking behind me, though don't take in what they're saying. I finish my set and get up. The taweez twink has his back and bubble butt to me. I am about to tap him on the shoulder to let him know I am finished when he bends his knees slightly and rests his hands on his knees. He is maybe just relaxing or stretching while talking to his friend, but he is positioned – and he must be aware of this – just in front of me, his ass pushed towards my crotch.

I could fuck you, I hear myself saying in my mind, pakka.

'Excuse me, do you want to do a set?' I say out loud.

'I'm done. All yours,' he says, looking round and smiling.

I finish my sets, find a bench and wheel it to the barbell area. Hero with hairy chest and mooch is doing squats there. He adjusts his shorts, pulls the hems up towards his crotch, presumably to be able to squat better. It also reveals more muscled thigh, and the massive, still covered upper parts almost burst through the thin textile he has pulled up. He does a final set, then starts taking some weights off.

'Leave those last ones, please,' I say, 'and could you help me just lift the bar down to the floor?'

He takes one end, I take the other, and we lift it down together, squatting in unison. I appreciate the small moment of cooperation.

I lie down and roll the bar over my legs to rest in the crease of my hip. Hands holding it in position, shoulders resting on the bench behind me, I thrust my hips up, using my glutes and thigh muscles. After two sets I rest and enjoy the warm, almost burning, sensation in these large muscle groups.

'Excuse me, what is this good for?' It is the lady again.

'Glutes and thighs,' I say, standing up and touching them. I tell her about the barbell hip thrust, the technique and its benefits. Then I put away the weights and bar, and head to the changing room.

The door says 'Men' and, directly beneath, 'Push Slowly'. I

push slowly, but there are no men in here. I open my locker, take out my bag and automatically check my phone. I have received a Grindr message.

'Come shower, na?'

It was him, the darker daddy. I sit down and untie my gym shoes. Out of the corner of my eye I see two guys coming out of the shower, talking. It is the darker daddy and taweez twink. While talking to each other, daddy dries his crotch area, revealing some of the cock casually hanging there, and twink dries his bubble butt, even parting the ass cheeks a bit. Blood rushes to my cock. They notice me, the now sizeable bulge in my shorts, and smile at me. As I start to undress, someone else enters the changing room. Hero. He smiles at me too, then he undresses, facing me, holding my gaze. Both of us naked, I follow him into the shower.

Shredded Dates

Despite Bombay traffic I arrive almost on time and enter the bar, Capital Social, to find a hip crowd seated at long tables. I don't understand the trend. In a city that is already so overcrowded, why would anyone want to pay so much to eat and drink on top of each other like this? Worse still, why would anyone choose this for a first date? A first date, a gay one in a predominantly straight society to top it off, is awkward enough as it is. I take a quick look at the Grindr photos that I have saved on my camera roll, find one of his face, put the phone away, and look up to see him waving at me from a packed table.

He is good-looking. V-shaped and muscled in a tight T-shirt. A nice smile. A perfectly symmetrical face. He says hi and something more in a baritone bordering on bass. My hand feels good in his, skin against skin. I pick up a masculine scent, woody and spicy. There is already a chemistry between us.

We sit down, facing each other, people on both sides of us, and look at the menu.

'Anything you recommend?' I ask.

'All their drinks are good,' he says.

I can't choose, too many choices. 'What are you having?' I ask.

'A double gin and tonic.'

'Maybe I should have one of their signatures. Aacharoska sounds different.' I look at him.

'I think Indian lime pickle sounds too much in a drink, but go ahead.'

'Maybe you're right. I'll go for something safer, maybe just rum and coke.'

He calls for the waiter.

'No, I think I'll have the same as you, double gin and tonic. Easy.'

He orders for us.

'You know how the American ideal is freedom of choice,' I say. 'The more choices, the better, right? I guess it's increasingly the ideology across the world, including India.'

He nods and looks at me attentively.

'I recently read these studies that suggest the opposite, that the more alternatives we are presented with, the less happy and more discontented we become,' I continue. 'Like just now I chose that double gin and tonic, but while I'm drinking it I'll wonder whether the lime pickle drink was in fact better. If they'd only had that signature drink, I wouldn't have had to spend energy choosing in the first place and later worrying whether it was the right choice. I would have just enjoyed that drink.'

He looks at me. Baffled perhaps. I don't know what he is thinking. I plough on:

'I probably spend more time choosing where and what to drink or eat than it takes the average traditional Indian to choose a spouse out of the alternatives given to them.'

I laugh a little bit. He does too, perhaps only because my laughter was a cue. At least he did. He joined me. He didn't leave me alone with my research rant and overly wordy half-jokes. Anyway, he might as well get to know my particular neuroses from the start, not least my issues with choosing and wanting to understand things in depth, the two possibly connected.

'But you seem to be able to choose quickly,' I add.

'I know what I want,' he says and looks me directly in the eyes. I get a hard-on and smile and lower my eyes.

'I like France,' I say. 'In restaurants there they often have only one vegetarian option; I don't have to choose. But it's changing there too. More vegetarianism, sadly.'

'So you're vegetarian?' he asks.

'Yeah. You?'

'No, I'm pure non-veg. I love my meat.'

'Okay.'

'Opposites attract, I guess,' he says.

He doesn't seem bothered by the people around us, and it attracts me that he is so confident and relaxed on a first date with a man among so many straight strangers. They must understand what is happening here. His being so relaxed about it makes me more relaxed. I can join him; we can be two, stronger, at our ease. I like myself with him.

'So what line of work are you in?' I ask.

'I'm a hunter,' he says, and it's a little ridiculous how he is trying to make himself interesting, but it's also charming. As he says it, he again looks me in the eyes. I know intellectually that this is a domination technique typical of males, conscious or not, but right now a hard-on is my automatic reaction, and I lower my eyes – a submission technique, conscious or not – and long for him to fuck me. Am I being hunted? I think I like it.

'It's sales jargon,' he continues. 'I'm a seller.'

'Oh. Tell me more.'

'There are hunters and farmers. Hunters typically want to close as many new and big deals as fast as possible. Farmers cultivate longer-term customer relationships.'

Hunter is definitely sexiest. And having just arrived in Bombay, going on Grindr here, I am a new and big deal. But I also want a longer-term relationship at some point. And I want to feel special.

'So have you been hunting men much?' I ask in a low voice, leaning in closer to him.

'I only realised I like men a couple of years ago. But I've had my share of random sex,' he says, without lowering his own voice. 'I want something more stable now.'

The drinks arrive. 'Cheers,' he says and raises his glass.

'Cheers,' I say, look him in the eyes, take a sip – gin and tonic, it is just fine – and put the glass down.

'So what exactly do you sell?' I ask.

'Data analytics. We sell information to businesses so they can understand customer preferences and behaviour better.'

'Sometimes I wonder if businesses understand me better than I do myself,' I say. 'The amount of information Facebook must have, for example.'

'Yeah. Facebook has assured its users that information is shared only with their permission and anonymised when sold on. But issues still arise with privacy settings not being clearly explained or too complex. Now tell me more about you, handsome. I've gathered from Facebook,' he laughs a little at this, 'that you're a psychologist, currently living in France, here for research, right?'

Maybe I should take the link to Facebook off my Grindr profile, I think to myself.

'Yeah,' I say, 'I left India for France fifteen years ago to study. Then I did a doctorate there and have stayed on, working in academia. I'm here to do some research on Indian gay life. Didi, my cousin sister, has a place in South Bombay. I'm staying with her for a month. Then I'm off to Delhi.'

'You look around mid-twenties, but you've done so much already,' he says. 'How old are you?'

'I'm thirty-four.'

'I would never have guessed.'

'You?'

'I'll be twenty-six this Sunday.'

This might help explain his relaxed attitude and audacity, I think to myself. He grew up and became a man during the LGBT-positive Naz-petition and judgment. I should make some field notes later. He looks at me, again that penetrating look, and I smile even more and look down, fixing my gaze on the drink but still watching him out of the corner of my eye.

'Why are you smiling?' he asks.

'It's the way you're looking at me.'

'I want you.'

'Hunter.'

'A good hunter. And I'm excellent in bed.'

'So confident,' I say, laughing, sensing my ass pushing a little back on the seat, my cock swelling, reacting to his words, wanting him.

'I love that,' he says.

'What?'

'You're biting your lips.'

I finish my drink in a single swallow. 'I think I'm already a little tipsy.'

'Good. Let's go somewhere else.'

He asks for the bill and insists on paying.

Outside it is getting dark but is still Bombay-warm and humid. We are standing face to face, less than an arm's length apart.

'Are you hungry?' he asks.

'Not really,' I say, 'but I'll come with you and have another drink and you can eat.'

'I'm okay. I want to eat you.' He looks me up and down; I am wearing short chino shorts that hug my butt and crotch.

I laugh.

'That means yes?' he asks.

At this point – partly intentionally and partly automatical-ly, I think – I get a look on my face that an ex described as 'eyes and smile that are so innocent and virgin-like, yet at the same time invite a guy to just fuck you hard here and now.'

'Let's go to my place,' he says. 'It's in Bandra.'

I nod.

He gets us an Uber and we climb in the back. A new Bolly-wood song is playing. He puts an arm around me; I make myself smaller and lean in to rest my head between his chest and upper-arm, his masculine scent more striking here. I look up at him. He looks down at me and smiles.

After a while we get stuck in traffic.

'Okay to walk the rest?' he asks. 'It's not too far.'

'Sure.'

As we walk amidst the bustle of cars and rickshaws and hawkers, his hand touches mine, then holds it. As we cross the road, or when we make a turn, he places a hand on my shoul-der, my lower back or around my waist, to guide me in the right direction, but surely primarily to touch me and be the one steering me, perhaps also marking me as his. I like it.

I think of how the body has its own logic. The smell, the touch, the taste and the voice of the other attracts us and motivates us strongly on a bodily, less conscious level. And often the body does know best who we are compatible with sexually. I give myself over to him moving me in the direction of his flat. I surrender to my body and his; no need to con-sciously choose. I am a little wary of others, though; walking hand in hand used to be okay among Indian boys and men, merely indicating friendly affection, but I don't know how it is viewed now.

'It still doesn't raise suspicion, two guys walking hand in hand like this?'

'Perhaps more now, and more so among the middle and upper classes, like here in Bandra.'

'I think an unfortunate side-effect of the gay movement in a lot of western countries has been that any caressing touch between men is now seen as potentially homosexual, and therefore more loaded and difficult. I've seen some old photos of European men, straight men, from a hundred years back, in colourful clothes, sitting on each other's laps caressing each other. Now it wouldn't happen unless they were gay. It would be sad if India also changes like that.'

He briefly strokes my ass with his hand and says, 'I want you on my lap.' And then, while we are still moving, our bodies close, his hand brushes against my thigh, just where my shorts end, and he slides some fingers slightly up my shorts and says, 'But without clothes. And not as a straight man.'

Walking here, him touching me in public, talking like this, turns me on. To make it less obvious I put my hands in my pockets, but this must also look rather strange, walking with my hands in the pockets of my short shorts.

'You don't care what people think?' I say. 'I was impressed in the social as well, how you seemed so unbothered by those around us.'

'They don't feed me.'

Surely there is more – or less – to him than this confidence, but I allow myself, and him, the pleasure of the sexy illusion for now.

We arrive at a fancy Bandra west complex. He greets the watchmen and lift-wala, again apparently unaffected by the fact that they may very well guess what is going on.

His flat is impressive: spacious and light, Scandinavian-style, and smells clean, slightly citrusy.

'Wow,' I say.

'I'll give you the full tour later,' he says and pushes me up against a wall. 'Now focus on this.' He takes my hand and puts it on his crotch. Obediently I explore the contours of the cock through the material of his trousers.

'Sorry if I was too rough,' he says.

'I like that you're assertive,' I say.

'I have your permission then.' He lifts me up, I scissor my legs around his waist, and he carries me through to the bedroom and puts me down on a king-size bed.

I look up at him. He unzips, and his cock springs out, fully erect and hard. I want it. I bend forward and lick. I suck. I let it slip out and admire it again.

He smiles and pushes me so I am on my back. Assertive. He pulls my shorts and briefs down to my knees, not all the way off, so they restrict my movement. I am his prey. He flips me over onto my stomach, and I feel his warm hands gently spreading my ass cheeks, and then his tongue. This is all there is in the world right now, his tongue, my hole, this sensation.

'Stay,' he says and gets up.

I feel the air from the fan and the AC on my naked ass, then the sensation of lube. He lubes my hole with care, like he is preparing a dessert, for himself, for me. He turns me around again and removes my shorts and briefs. While looking directly in my eyes, that penetrating look, he slides one finger into my hole, then another. Eventually I don't know how many are in, but they are pressing the right spot with just the right force. I think I could come without even touching my cock, just his fingers in me like this.

'Oh my god,' I moan, 'this is so good.'

'I'll be the best lover you've ever had.'

'Yes.'

Then his fingers withdraw, and I feel the thick head of his cock against my hole.

Slowly he enters me.

'I like that,' he says.

'What?' I ask.

'You moaning so loudly.'

'Sorry. I wasn't even aware. Your neighbours – I should be quiet,' I say.

'Don't worry.'

Slowly he pulls almost all the way out, then pushes all the way in again, stays there. And then, while he is completely in, I sense his thick cock expanding even more, him doing something to make it even thicker. I sense the pressure against the elastic walls, him expanding me from the inside.

He takes my hands and pulls them up over my head, inviting me to surrender even more, and I gladly do, choosing not to choose for a while. My body responds to his, his body to mine.

He kisses and bites me on my neck and arms.

'Hunter,' I say.

'You're mine,' he says.

As he fucks me, the remnant of his perfume mixes with the scents of lube and pre-cum and sweat and citrus. It enters me, fills me, intoxicates me.

We fuck till exhaustion and rest for a while on the comfortable bed.

'Now I could eat some food,' he says. 'How about you?'

I nod.

'There's a place not far from here that I quite like. Pali Village Café,' he says. 'But it has mostly European cuisine. I don't know if you want that, just coming from Europe, though?'

'No, that's good. I trust you,' I say, appreciating both being asked and not having to decide.

We get dressed and go back out. On the way to the restaurant we pass a sabji-wala. Deep purple eggplants are piled up on his cart. 'Aloo, baingan, tamaatar,' he announces again and again.

'For a long time I didn't understand what all the eggplants were doing popping up on Grindr,' I say and laugh. 'The banana wasn't enough, I guess.'

'You can have as much as you want,' he says.

I think about the eggplant emoji on his Grindr profile and his actual cock. If not very long, his cock is certainly thick. But don't I want to try others, perhaps even bigger ones? I am only in Bombay for a little while. Walking past the eggplants and the young and beautiful men of Bandra, I feel more ambivalent about holding his hand.

And going to eat after sex, what does that mean? Am I promising him something more than I want to give? Sure, the sex was good, but good sex can be deceptive, I remind myself. With all the hormones released, you feel euphoric and deeply connected, and you become more attached. But how well would we actually match, apart from sexually? He is into sales and business. He can't go a day without eating meat. And his cockiness and assertiveness would surely get on my nerves eventually. I make him walk in front of me between a cart and some cars, ostensibly because of the street being too crowded to walk next to each other, but by doing so I can also let go of his hand.

We arrive at the restaurant: high ceiling, exposed walls, green plants, wood and iron furniture, flickering candles on the tables, separate tables spaced comfortably, thankfully. It is rustic and romantic; it makes me slightly uneasy. We look at the menus. There are several vegetarian options. He knows immediately what to order for himself, something non-veg. I discuss some options with him. When he says something pro one option, I find a con; when he says something con, I find a pro.

'I'm thinking maybe the warm kale salad with shredded dates. It sounds good,' I say. 'But so do the other two.'

'Yeah. I don't know about the combination of dates and kale,' he says.

I am getting irritable. I want to choose myself now. 'I think that sounds quite good,' I say. 'Yeah, I think I will have that one.'

It turns out to be warm kale, shredded dates, almonds, parmesan, lemon juice, and delicious.

'I'm going to my parents in Nashik this weekend,' he says. 'Come.'

'Would that be okay?'

'You could come as a friend, and then, while they're sleeping, I'll fuck you.'

'They don't know?'

'I'll tell them eventually, but they'll be disappointed. I'm the oldest son, and they expect me to take over the family business, and eventually that a grandson takes over. My father built the business from scratch. Growing up I knew hunger,' he says.

'I can understand that business and making money is important to you, then,' I say.

'Not really. My family has taught me that people and experiences like this, to sit here and be together with you, are more important. Money comes and goes. Come with me? I could show you Nashik. It's a city with soul, not transactional like Mumbai.'

'You go often?' I ask, trying to dodge the invitation with a question that could be interpreted as indicating that I might come another time.

'Once a month or so. I'm going now because it's my birthday.'

'Oh yeah. That's right. Any birthday wishes?'

'You,' he says quickly without smiling or laughing, just the penetrating look. I smile and laugh a little.

'Do you want anything else to eat or drink?' he asks as we finish our meals.

'I think I'm good.'

'And you have to leave some space for me.' He smiles. 'We can go back to my place, fuck a bit more, and then you can spend the night.'

'That would be nice. But I think I should head back to Didi. I only arrived a couple of days ago, and we made plans to spend all day tomorrow together.'

'I understand.' He asks for the bill.

'Let me pay now,' I say. 'You paid for those over-priced drinks at the social.'

I insist on paying.

'There are taxis just down the road,' he says as we leave the restaurant.

He walks with me, and we stop near a line of taxis waiting for customers. He moves close, brushes up against me.

'I want you,' he says. 'I know you're only here for a little while, but be mine for four weeks, and then we can see.'

It doesn't sound like such a bad deal: four weeks' trial and then we can see, and the sex was certainly good. But I am only in Bombay for a little while; what about others I might meet through Grindr? I simply smile at him.

'I'll take you to the moon every night,' he continues.

Experiencing him like this, having told me about his family, promising me things, waiting for an answer, almost begging me, I sense sides of him other than the hunter and the cockiness. He wants to love and be loved. And I wish that for him. But, while I do feel something for him, I don't know if I want to commit, even for these four weeks.

'But you've just started meeting men,' I say. 'Only a couple of years ago, you said.'

'So?'

'Well, there are so many more to meet.'

'I told you: I want something more stable.'

Grindr is a bit like the drink and food menus with all their beguiling options, I think to myself. He is one of the first guys I meet in Bombay. I have already received a lot of messages, including dick pics, some of them quite impressive, from other guys, and some of them seem interesting and might be good matches. On the other hand I know that no one is going to be perfect. Perhaps I should just say yes to the four weeks. I wonder if this is the seller in him, somehow knowing how to work me. But perhaps, in a way that is somewhat similar to the businesses that benefit from the analysis of big data, he does know better than me, seeing something in himself and in me that I don't.

'So is that a yes? You can still leave the taxi and come back to my place.'

'That would be nice. But Didi is expecting me, and . . .'

'I understand.'

We hug, he gives me a quick kiss on my neck, and I get in a waiting taxi.

While being driven to Didi's my phone beeps with a text message: he has sent me a kiss and a heart. I feel an ache. I don't know what to do. Almost automatically I log onto Grindr, this blessing and curse. My phone beeps again, and I read the text.

'Call 55315. Yadi koi bhi pareshani hai toh paye samadhan Panditji se turant at Rs9/min.'

My first reaction is irritation that the phone company is allowing these ads to be sent to my number. Then, for a moment, I actually wonder if consulting a Hindu astrologer might be a way to get a clear answer and direction. Even if it is not the right one, and not scientific by any means, at least it would be an answer from some apparent authority outside myself. But in the end I don't act on the offer.

The next day I take Didi all the way from South Bombay up to the same restaurant for lunch, Pali Village Café. He is probably at work at this time, I think to myself. But if I did bump into him it could seem to be by cosmic will. I would introduce him to Didi. I suppose I would say he is a friend – at least the first time they meet.

He is not here.

'They have a very good kale salad,' I tell Didi.

We look at the menus. I don't see it, so I ask the waiter.

'We have taken it off the menu, sir.'

'Since yesterday?!' I say. 'Why?'

'Good that you had it the other night then,' Didi says.

Fucking Delhi

D

Delhi. Dirty. Loud. Rude. Violent. Delhi, 'Scam City', has cheated me and picked my pockets. Delhi, 'Rape Capital', has pushed and shoved and groped me – female friends recount much worse experiences. Upon returning from my few and brief visits I would have complained endlessly, were it not for the pollution leaving me almost without voice. And yet I have decided to give this sisterfucking city another chance. Literature can redeem even Delhi.

What triggers my current visit is an invitation to a queer poetry event. It is an opportunity to present and discuss my most recent book, which explores a homoerotic meeting between a Hindu boy and Jesus. When booking my flight I remember D. I text him that I will be coming for the poetry event and hope we can meet up. He immediately texts back that he is out of town that day, 'but hopefully we can meet the next day or so?'

I start typing, 'Sadly I'll be returning to Bombay the same evening,' but then I stop myself. I fell in love with Bombay years ago, and have made it my second home. Many like to hate Delhi, but no one more than Bombay folks. I guess it is partly an identity thing, how we define our small selves, us versus them, but friendship and literature can challenge narrow views and reveal the complexities of people and places. I have D, who I have not seen in a long time, and I have many books set in Delhi on my list of things to read – and I like to read books in the places where they are set. Maybe I can even offer my own readers a Delhi-based story. Maybe a homoerotic meeting between a Bombay guy and Delhi is what is needed now.

I decide to stay a couple of extra days, book my flight, and message D again. I tell him I will try to find a place in Greater Kailash, the same neighbourhood as the poetry venue, an area I have not stayed in before. He messages me the website of a gay boutique hotel located there, adding, 'if nothing else it might inspire some stories' and a crazy face emoji with stuck-out tongue and winking eye.

I check out the website of The Mister & Art House. They present themselves as a 'Boutique Luxury Guesthouse for GAY MEN ONLY', all in pink, and with the last three words in capital letters. There is a sexually suggestive photo of two guys in the shower together. Another shows a seating area with dark wooden furniture and antique-style art. And then there are some photos of rather ridiculous homoerotic art, including a painting of a very ripped Krishna in a tiny loincloth. 'Could be fun,' I message D back, and make a reservation. Included in the standard welcoming email is an offer for 'a full-body massage by a GAY male massage therapist.'

E

E, an employee of the hotel, meets me at the airport and takes my small suitcase. He is lanky like Indian ladkas can be. He has full lips, and when he smiles they reveal a set of white teeth, all in order.

I remember Delhi being either scorching hot or freezing cold. But now, as we exit the airport building, I notice how pleasant the temperature is, and the air is smooth against my skin. Timing is important for any relationship, I guess. It is March, and the first time I experience Delhi in spring.

He leads me to a taxi. We get in, and I rest my head and close my eyes. It was an early morning flight, and I am feeling a little unwell. I have been coughing for a couple of days, and last night I think I had a fever. Occasionally I hear E and the driver talking to each other; occasionally I open my eyes a little. I catch a glimpse of large trees that are bare except for some fiery red flowers, palash I believe.

'We've arrived, sir,' E says, touching my shoulder lightly,

waking me up.

I get out of the car. It is a quiet, green, obviously posh area. We enter a building which seems to be mainly residential, and take the lift to the third floor. E leads me through a door into the guesthouse lobby and proceeds to give me a tour of the adjacent sitting and dining rooms. 'This is where breakfast is served.' The place is quite cosy and as the website photos promised. An art piece that stands out is a sculpture made up of different-sized penises offered on cupped palms. We return to the lobby, off which are doors to the separate guestrooms, and E opens the door to the one where I will be staying.

'Do you want to order the massage?'

'I don't think so. Not now in any case. Thanks.'

I go in, lock the door, lie down on the bed and check my phone. The poetry event is in a couple of hours. I have time to rest a bit. But first I log on to Grindr. I write in the 'About me' section, 'Come join me and other queer poets at the Tabula Beach Café today at 3.30.' I change my photo to one where I am shirtless – and leaner than I am today. It feels somewhat cheap. But sex sells. And my book is homoerotic, so it is not exactly misleading. And I am curious about Delhi guys and sex. A nearby top calls himself 'XL guy'. His profile pic reveals a handsome face. I send him a hi.

I sleep for an hour, shower, feel slightly better, and take an Uber to Tabula Beach Café. The outside seating area is carpeted with fine sand, giving the place a chilled Goa vibe. Inside there is a long bar, and then a separate room where some people are arranging chairs in rows facing a small stage. I spot the organiser of the event and walk up to her. It is the first time we meet live. She is a woman in her late thirties, with very short hair and a smile that could make her seem carefree and confident but does not convince me.

'I liked the questions and topics for our conversation that you emailed me,' I say, trying to build some rapport.

'Good,' she says. 'Just let me know if there are any other things you want to talk about.'

'Well,' I say, 'I think the book also raises the issue of hook-up apps like Grindr, the possibilities and challenges that come with them.'

'Yeah. I think that's quite male-centric though,' she says

with a tight smile, 'and I want this to be as inclusive as possible.'

'Oh. Okay,' I say, 'I guess we already have enough to talk about anyway.' I tense my face muscles, pushing my lips up into a smile that must be as fake as hers. 'I'll just go use the washroom before we start.'

I find the toilet, unzip, take out my cock and pee. She has read my book. And she invited me here. And now she tells me *male-centric*! What the fuck! Delhi elites, politically correct and narrow-minded like no other! *Inclusive*?! What does she think, that inclusion merely means an inversion of hierarchy, the marginalisation of cis-males?

I take a copy of my book, which I've marked up for my reading, out of my shoulder bag. It starts with the narrator logging on to Grindr and finding a top with a big cock who fucks him. I had planned to start there. What can I find that would be okay to read here? I sigh, put the book away, wash my hands and come back out.

The room is filling up with mostly women and a few people with a more androgynous look. I sit on one of the audience chairs and look through the book again.

'Hi.' A guy sitting nearby leans over.

'Hi,' I say, pleasantly surprised to realise it is XL guy. I see now that he is XL in body size; it may not be a reference to his cock at all. And while I can like a manly paunch, I think this guy is a bit too big for my sexual preference.

'I tried to message you back on Grindr,' he says. 'I was wondering whether this was free. Then I just took a chance and came.'

'I'm glad,' I say. And I really am, not least because he has just significantly added to the percentage of cis-men in the crowd. 'You have an interest in poetry?' I continue.

'I do,' he says.

The organiser comes up to me. 'We should get on stage for the conversation.'

'Talk later,' I say to XL guy.

The book is what it is, I think to myself as I step onto the stage. If the audience here doesn't like it, it can't be helped: I can't pretend it is something else. I don't want to go into some closet – at a queer poetry event, at that.

The organiser says a few introductory words about her organisation, the event and me. Then she asks me a question about love. I am not sure what the question was exactly but I start speaking.

'The narrator of this story is a gay man searching for love in the age of hook-up apps,' I say. 'Let me read something so you all get an impression of where he starts in his journey, the intense longing he feels and how he attempts to address it.'

I open the book and read from the start:

'"Chest pain, gut pang / Want to / Be wanted / Skin against / Skin / Long to / Be held / Be filled / Belong / Log on to / Grindr / New guy nearby / Top / Hot enough / Hi / Share some more pics? / I hope for / Big dick / It is / Wow / Now?"'

If the organiser is irritated, she doesn't let it show. She asks me a question about being queer and spiritual. We have a good conversation.

During the break I take out some other copies of my book from the shoulder bag and sit down near the stage, hoping for sales. XL guy is first in line.

'Shall I write something in it?' I ask.

'Please.'

'What's your name again?'

He tells me, and I write 'Dear', his name, 'Enjoy', sign it and give it to him.

'I have to leave now, but I'm glad I met you. Where are you staying in Delhi?' he asks.

'GK2.'

'Me too. I can show you around.'

'Thanks. I'm only here for a couple of days, but let's stay in touch and see what's possible,' I say. I look at the others waiting behind him. 'I should talk to these people now.'

'Sure. I'll text you.'

'Okay. And thanks again for coming.'

I smile and look at my book in his hand. He smiles, turns and walks away. He didn't pay. Was the book my payment to him for coming to watch me?

'I loved it,' says a thin girl, and takes out some money to buy a copy.

'Thanks,' I say, pleasantly surprised to see a girl here who appreciated it, and feeling more confident that while the book is homoerotic and describes a particular experience, there is something universal in there, longing and love, that everyone can relate to.

'Can I give you a hug?' she asks.

'Sure.'

She hugs me with her thin, bony arms and thin, bony torso, and her thin, bony face brushes my cheek. I soften.

'God bless you,' she says, smiling.

'God bless you too,' I respond, also smiling.

After a few more conversations and books sold, I find my seat in the audience and watch the next set of poets. An androgynous girl performs a poem about her experience of being androgynous; her whole body speaks it, every muscle, every movement. Next is a poet who identifies as a transman. Then one who identifies as a femme lesbian. I enjoy the performances. I also remember that much of the movement and the community, both queer and literary, has been dominated by cis-males. I appreciate the need for other perspectives. Now that I have been open here about who I am, a cis-male with an interest in cocks, I can sit back and enjoy the other poets and their perspectives. This is unity in diversity. This is inclusive.

'How did it go, sir?' E asks me, back at the hotel.

'Quite well,' I say.

E smiles his nice smile.

'Are you interested in poetry?' I ask him.

'Sometimes.'

Just below his lips is a chin dimple. What is it that makes chin dimples so attractive? Is it the suggestion of something sexual and sometimes even dirty – the ass – in a place where one is otherwise so presentable and clean – the face? Like some people's obsession with Mormon porn: smooth-skinned young men with short hair so neatly combed, dressed in suits, and then one fucks the other in the ass, he begs for more, they come, and the clothes and hair are all over the place, dishevelled.

I look at E, his lips, his clean-shaven face, the chin dimple. I am getting a hard-on. I could fuck him. I hope that a small smile is a suitable response to whatever he has been saying for the past couple of minutes. He stops talking and smiles back.

'Would you like dinner, sir?'

'I'm okay for now. Thanks.'

I enter my room, take off my clothes, lie down on the bed and start reading Khushwant Singh's *Delhi*.

I read about how, from around the year 1000, North India was raided quite regularly by nomadic Turks. Some settled and created a sultanate that was ruled from Delhi. The first sultan was Qutubuddin Aibak, and his name is still remembered through the Qutub Minar. I don't think I have ever actually seen the 240-feet tall tower. Perhaps I will this time.

I continue reading about various sultans, about Qutubuddin Mubarak Shah and Khusro Khan, a Hindu boy captured during an expedition in Gujarat. Allegedly the boy was fair, gazelle-eyed and had a nice ass. Qutubuddin coloured the boy's lips and put kohl on his eyes. I merge E with the captured boy in my mind and imagine myself as the sultan, the boy's coloured lips on my cock. I come and clean up. Then I order some food on Zomato – a paneer tandoori roti roll from Dilli BC – and continue reading.

After a while the sultan started colouring his own lips as well. He started letting the boy do to him what he had done to the boy. Many of his Muslim subjects were upset by that. The sultan thought they were unhappy because the boy was Hindu, so he was converted and renamed Khusro Khan. The two celebrated by getting drunk and frolicking in the open.

The Zomato app tells me my order is arriving. I put on some sports shorts and go down and out of the building to pick it up. On my way back, Zomato bag in hand, I see E sitting on the lobby sofa with some papers. He seems to be here a lot. I briefly smile at him, go back to my room, get out of the shorts and start eating the food naked in bed. I hold *Delhi* with my left hand, the roti roll in my right, the sauce getting my fingers sticky.

The two started role-playing. One evening Qutubuddin would arrive as a Turkish bridegroom, sign a contract of marriage with Khusro Khan, and take him to the sofa. The next evening Khusro Khan would arrive as a Rajput on horseback, find Qutubuddin dressed up as a Turkish bride, walk with him around a fire to the chanting of Hindu mantras, and take him to the sofa.

I imagine being dressed up as a Turkish bride, spider-web veil and fine silk clothes on my masculine body, then being disrobed and fucked by the boy. I come again, this time on the Zomato bag.

Having finished my meal and come twice, I am starting to feel sleepy, but I want to finish the chapter.

On one of the evenings on the sofa, when Khusro Khan was the bridegroom and Qutubuddin the bride, Khusro Khan was holding onto the sultan's cock and balls as he fucked him from behind. Overcome with passion, he rammed his cock harder and harder into him and crushed his balls in his hand. After Khusro Khan came he cut off the sultan's head. Then he reconverted back to Hinduism and proclaimed himself sultan. In less than a year, however, he was defeated in a battle and himself beheaded.

I think about the poetry event and what I have just read and fantasised about. I think about identities, power, passion and role-play. I try to follow a line of thinking, come to some conclusion, but I am tired. Imagining that I have been beheaded, I soon fall asleep.

L

'Lodhi Gardens?'

I wake up to some messages from D, asking how the poetry event went and suggesting we meet in the evening, in Lodhi Gardens. It is not too far, and I have never been there before. I text D back, agreeing. I look it up and find out that the Lodhis were the last sultans of Delhi. I start thinking about sultans, boys and sex again. I jerk off, shower and get dressed.

E is in the lobby, just outside my room, again – or still. Does he sleep here?

'Good morning, sir. Breakfast is ready.'

I follow him to a large, wooden dining table. There are aloo pakoras, anda bhurji and more set out, but only one plate, one cup, one glass and one set of cutlery.

'All this for me? No other guests?'

'Some left yesterday. Some arrive later today. This is all for you, sir,' E says and smiles. 'Chai ya coffee?'

'Coffee please.'

He pours me a cup. Instant coffee. I make myself say, 'Thanks.'

E hovers over me while I eat. Maybe I hurt his feelings by ordering food on Zomato last night. But with Zomato I can choose anything I want, and it is more reasonable than the hotel menu. I guess his boss wants him to sell as much as possible, dinners, massages and what not.

'You used to go to the gym?' he asks.

I am wearing a T-shirt, biceps veins still visible.

'Yeah.'

'But you don't go anymore?'

'I haven't been in a few weeks.'

'I can tell.'

I laugh. He doesn't. Was that just the kind of directness that you will sometimes get here, no malice intended? Or just plain Delhi rudeness? I take a bite of an aloo pakora. It is dry and tasteless. I consider telling him but don't. I leave it on my plate and start googling for breakfast and coffee places nearby. Carnatic Café is highly recommended. 'The best South Indian food joint in Delhi.' 'Best filter coffee in the city.' Fifteen minutes' walk away, in M Block Market, according to Google Maps.

'I'm done,' I say. 'Thank you.'

'No more?' E asks incredulously.

'I have an appointment to meet someone,' I lie.

Outside the temperature is still very pleasant. It is surprisingly clean, not too many people, not too polluted. I realise this is a much nicer neighbourhood than I have ever stayed in before in Delhi. I am a little older and better off. And I guess Delhi is a whore like any other city: you get what you pay for.

Lining the road down to M Block Market are large palash trees. The trees themselves are completely naked, no leaves, just scarlet flowers. Some have fallen on the road and I step over them. They lie around looking almost obscene, out in the open, so plump, fleshy and red.

I arrive at Carnatic Café, a simple yet warm place. I find myself a corner table and sit. There are only a few other customers at this time. I order a milky filter coffee, a coconut dosa and sambar. Then I log on to Grindr and find some messages from XL guy. I don't reply. I look through the other messages and guys. Some are sexy, and I send a few messages. When the food arrives I put my phone away. They are playing Carnatic music, slow singing and strings, non-intrusive. I enjoy the music and the food. Then I order a black coffee with cardamom and continue reading *Delhi*.

I read about how the rise of Sufism accompanied the sultanate. I read about Nizamuddin, the Sufi saint who lived in the late thirteenth to early fourteenth century. He was accused of heresy and summoned by the sultan to account for himself.

'Is it true that you don't distinguish between Muslims and Hindus?' the sultan asked.

'It's true,' Nizamuddin answered, 'I consider both Muslims and Hindus children of God. And the best way to serve God is through love of His creatures.'

Nizamuddin believed there are innumerable names for God and ways to approach God. Your path may lead to the mosque or the temple, to a place full of people or a solitary cave in the wilderness. What's important is how you walk the path, that you walk with love.

I think about love in the age of hook-up apps. I check Grindr again, read the messages from XL guy. I thank him for coming yesterday and for his offer to show me around. I tell him I probably won't be able to squeeze him in this time. I hope I am kind. I log off and return to my book.

Another charge against Nizamuddin had to do with dancing and music.

'Is it true that you and your followers engage in this?' the sultan asked.

'When God's grace enters one's person it manifests itself by making that person sing and dance with joy,' Nizamuddin answered.

Many were drawn to him. There is one who stands out: Amir Khusro, a Sufi mystic and poet. 'You made me your bride when our eyes met,' Amir Khusro said. Together they sang, danced and loved. Amir Khusro wrote poetry and songs about it.

I remain here for several hours, reading *Delhi*, writing some notes for a possible story, drinking strong coffee, listening to soft music, slowly falling in love with this city.

In the early evening I take an Uber to Lodhi Gardens. D

waits for me by the entrance. As we hug I pick up his scent – clean, not heavily perfumed, more like some mild soap, like he has just showered. His soft, slightly plump body is covered by a loose shirt with a flowery pattern. His hair is shoulder-length and coloured fiery red. I remember that he teaches Queerness in Literature at a university here.

'This is new?' I say, nodding towards the hair. 'It reminds me of some flowers I keep seeing here. Palash, na?'

'Yeah,' he says. 'There used to be forests of palash here. Still there are many trees scattered around the city.' His voice is gentle.

'They're beautiful,' I say. 'And so is your hair.'

'Many consider the flower a symbol of spring and love,' he says.

We enter the gardens, follow a footpath, and are soon surrounded by extensive lawns and all sorts of trees and flowers. I notice neems, ashokas, gulmohars, palms, marigolds, dahlias, phlox and countless others. I take a deep breath.

'The lungs of Delhi,' D says and smiles at me.

It is serene yet full of life. A group of people is doing yoga on the grass. A family is having a picnic, surrounded by squirrels begging for a bite of their food. On a bench a man lies resting; next to him lies a stray dog, also resting. A peacock shows off his iridescent blue and green plumage. A woodpecker is busy feasting on something on a tamarind tree. And scattered around the gardens are impressive domes constructed of red, grey and black sandstone, the tombs of the Lodhis and other sultans I assume. We approach one of them.

'This is the Shisha Gumbad, the Glazed Dome, so called because it was originally decorated with shining blue tiles,' D tells me. 'A few still remain. See?' He points up at some traces of brilliant blue.

'Shall we sit?' he asks. I nod, and we sit down on the broad steps leading up to the entrance.

Facing us at the other end of a garden, and raised on a platform, is an even larger dome, a hundred feet or so high at its apex.

'Bara Gumbad,' D says, 'the Big Dome.'

A young couple, dressed up beautifully, newly-weds I guess, are posing in the garden with the tomb as a backdrop.

Coming in our direction are two middle-aged men, hand in hand. They are quite fair, well-nourished it seems, judging from what I can see of their bodies, and wear designer sports clothes, all of which makes me conclude that they are middle to upper class, and that walking hand in hand probably means they are more than friends. D and I exchange glances, knowingly, as they pass by.

'Lodhi Gardens is gay-friendly then?' I say.

'Well, it's not a cruising spot, but yeah, it's quite popular among queers,' D says, looking in their direction.

'Thanks for helping me fall more in love with Delhi,' I say.

'My pleasure,' D says. 'So how did the poetry event go yesterday?'

'After a bumpy start it went very well,' I say.

I recount some of my experiences before asking him about life at the university. He tells me about his course and his students, the good and bad of #MeToo and trigger warnings, and trying to teach sexuality and gender in that context. He talks about new books he is reading and having his students read.

'I'll try to include your book on the reading list.'

'Better have a trigger warning then,' I say, and we chuckle. 'I'm flattered,' I continue.

'Are you currently reading anything interesting?' he asks me.

'Khushwant Singh's *Delhi*. I was reading about Nizamuddin and Amir Khusro,' I say.

'Their shrines, their dargahs, are not so far from here, you know. And there is qawwali there in the evening. It is one of my favourite places in Delhi. We can go if you want?'

'Oh, yes! Please.'

Immersed in conversation I only half-noticed two women come up the steps. They walked past us into the Shisha Gumbad. Something felt slightly off. I'm not sure what it was; they could have just been a pair of North-Indian, somewhat masculine-looking, middle-aged women. One turned and looked at D as she went inside. I think she said something. Had she reacted negatively to his appearance, his gender-bending? But she did smile.

'What just happened with that lady?'

'She blessed me,' D says.

'What did she say?'

'"Jiyo." May you live. May you be happy,' he says. 'People often think of hijras as aggressive and all of that, but you noticed how sweetly she smiled and spoke to me.'

'Ah. I didn't realise they were hijras. They knew you were queer then?'

'Yeah. They never take money from me.'

D and I remain on the steps for a while, catching up, and then, in a more meditative silence, just looking out at the tomb and the gardens. Suddenly a group of birds take off from the dome, flapping their wings, ascending into the blue evening sky.

'We should probably go now to be there in time for the qawwali,' D says, 'if you want to?'

'Yes.'

We leave the gardens. D hails an auto-rickshaw, negotiates a price, and after a few minutes' drive we arrive at a village-like mohalla. I see men with beards, kurtas and namaz skullcaps. No one seems to mind us, not even gender-bending D; perhaps they are used to a diverse crowd coming to the dargahs. There is a smell of grilled meat. I turn and see kebabs and other street food in the stalls.

'This is one of the oldest areas of Delhi,' D tells me as I follow him through a labyrinth of alleys.

Small hole-in-the-wall shops sell prayer books, mats, beads, skullcaps and fragrant roses and other flowers. All around us – hanging from wires, kept neatly folded or displayed in the shops – are chadars in violet, red, green, yellow, embroidered with sparkling golden threads. We stop at a shop where D buys some roses. We also leave our sandals there – the shops offer that service for free to the pilgrims – and continue barefoot.

Eventually we pass through an archway, and see the dargah of Amir Khusro: a small, timeworn building of red sandstone topped by a marble dome. D tells me he will wait outside, that he has been many times, but that I should enter. He gives me the roses.

In the middle, taking up most of the intimate space, is Amir Khusro's grave, which looks almost like a bed. It is covered by chadars and strewn with flowers – roses, marigolds and jasmines. Two young men have brought a delicate chadar with them. I watch as they take one end each and gently lift it into place as if they are putting someone to bed, tucking him in. I lay some roses on top of the chadar. The walls and ceiling are covered in multi-coloured geometrical shapes, floral patterns and calligraphy. There is a lamp in the middle of the ceiling; a fan just beneath it makes the light flicker. Apart from the whispering prayers of the few men in here, there is only the sound of the fan. Then I hear the call to prayer, 'Allahu Akbar', long a, liquid l. It must be from a nearby mosque. The muezzin sings it beautifully. It almost moves me to tears, the sounds themselves, the sincerity of the singer, the reminder that God is great, the longing and love. I am still not well from my cold, fever, whatever it is. It makes me more vulnerable and open to everything, inside and outside. I have fewer defences against the divine. I say a silent prayer.

D is waiting for me outside. We stand and look at the small dargah without speaking, surrounded by other pilgrims and the call to prayer. I notice a boy standing near the entrance to the dargah, maybe in his late teens. He looks around a little, catches me watching him. I think he likes it: he keeps looking to see if I am looking, with curiosity, with anxiety, with excitement. He has an innocence about him. His fair skin, still largely untainted by sun and suffering, contrasts with his black kurta and raven hair. He pulls up the trousers a little, revealing calves that are small but succulent, and even whiter than his face, rasgulla white. He comes towards us, a phone in his hand. I hold my breath: is he coming to confront me, did I misinterpret his signs, is he upset by my looking? No. He turns to take some photos of the dargah. I want to stand behind him and wrap my larger arms and body around his little body. I think of the love between men, between older and younger, between teacher and disciple, spiritual love, carnal love.

'Shall we go to Nizamuddin's?' D suggests. I nod.

We walk around Amir Khusro's dargah, and there it is, Nizamuddin's, only a short distance between them. Nizamuddin, the older man and teacher, has a bigger dargah. The square chamber sits on a platform and is surrounded by ornamental arches and pillars. Everything is covered in floral patterns and calligraphy, and the walls of the chamber itself have filigreed screens set into them. Crowning it is an onion dome in white marble with black-marble stripes. I enter – it is a similar room to Amir Khusro´s, only much bigger – and walk around the grave. When I come back out again the namaz is ending. I notice that the mosque lies on one side of the court-yard. There is whispering more than calling now, just a word here and there, and then nothing.

The day is quickly turning to night, and lights come on around the dargahs. An old man appears with a harmonium. He sits on the ground facing Nizamuddin's dargah, his back to Amir Khusro's. He starts playing and singing. The old man's voice is frail, but they are Amir Khusro's words, and the music, qawwali, is Amir Khusro's creation. The old man raises a hand, stretching out towards Nizamuddin as if he is Amir Khusro. We sit down behind him, facing Nizamuddin as if we too are Amir Khusro. A large man with a tabla sits next to the harmonium-player, his fat fingers fluent on the tight skin of the drums. An older lady offers some money to the musicians, then sits down behind them. She is elegantly dressed in a yellow sari. I notice a line of red sindoor where she has parted her hair. A married Hindu woman. The young boy in the black kurta appears and sits down close to me. From the corner of my eye I notice that he occasionally looks at me. More and more people join us. Again, no one seems to mind D and his gender-bending look.

'It makes me so happy,' I say to him. 'This mixed group of people coming together, of all religions, genders, sexualities, ages.'

D smiles back. 'We're a gathering of lovers.'

We sit for half an hour or so, listening, occasionally joining in the singing. I start to feel weak and slightly dizzy. Eventually I decide I should get back to the hotel and rest. I tell D. We get to our feet and leave the boy in the black kurta and the rest of the group. D follows me out of the mohalla back onto the main road, and waits with me there till the Uber arrives.

In the car I start wondering if what I have is more than a common cold. A couple of weeks ago I came across a guy on Grindr proudly declaring that he had an eight-incher. I invited him over to my house in Bandra. He was not very good-looking, but there was still the promise of that eight-incher. Jeans and boxers came off. His cock was okay, not eight. I still felt I owed him a fuck though; he had come all the way from across town, after all. I said we could go bareback since I was on PrEP. He pushed into me; I milked him a little by squeezing my ass while he was inside me. He held me tight and said stop and pulled out. He told me I made him so horny he would come any minute. I would be happy if he did; I didn't feel I owed him a long fuck. I said nothing, merely smiled seductively. He put his cock back in, I continued my milking trick, and soon he came. We small-talked for a few minutes. Then I said I had to get back to work, and he left. I went to the toilet and pushed his sperm back out and showered. Maybe that's it, I think to myself in the Uber; I may have caught an STD. I should go for a test when I am back in Bombay.

Back at the hotel I meet E, who as usual is in the lobby. He asks me about my day. I tell him about Lodhi Gardens and the dargahs. I ask if he has been there himself. He has not; he has been busy working since he moved to Delhi five years ago. He asks if I would like dinner tonight. I tell him I will just order on Zomato. As I am about to enter my room the door next to mine opens, and a white guy with a shaved head, wearing just boxers, appears. He smiles and says hi to me, then turns to E and asks for water.

I make an order on Zomato, this time from The Gourmet's, a veg thali with dhal, paneer, romali roti, jeera rice, and their special winter gajar ka halwa. Soon I hear E's voice just outside my door, and then the voice of what sounds like an Australian woman. Strange, I think to myself, in a 'GAY MEN ONLY' hotel. Perhaps the newcomer doesn't know. Perhaps E and the staff don't know how to handle the awkward situation.

I log on to Grindr. XL guy has messaged me 'no worries' and a smiley. Some of the sexy guys I messaged earlier have also messaged me back and seem interested. But I am too tired and unwell to meet up with anyone now. I think about the boy in the black kurta, his smooth and fair skin, his small hips. I jerk off and come. Soon after that the food arrives. The special gajar ka halwa is warm and red and not too sweet. I feel a little better and fall asleep.

H

'Humayun's tomb.'

I wake up to some new messages from D. He hopes I am feeling better, and suggests I go to the Mughal emperor's tomb if I wake up early. I look at the time on my phone; it's not even six yet. And I am feeling better. I think I have been to Humayun's tomb as a child, but that is a long time ago. And, according to D, it is best to go in the early morning. I can go now, I think to myself, and have breakfast somewhere nearby. I order an Uber and quickly get dressed. On my way out I bump into E.

'Up early, sir. Breakfast?' he asks.

'No, thanks. I'm going straight out.'

'Okay.'

I am about to leave but then remember the woman's voice from yesterday. I am curious about what happened. I turn to him and say in Hindi, 'Yesterday you had some new guests arrive?'

He does the Indian headshake.

'A woman guest as well?'

He continues the Indian headshake.

'But this hotel is only for gay men, no?'

'He can also come, sir,' E says. 'Trans man,' he adds in English in a lower voice.

'Ah,' I say. 'Achcha.' I smile.

The Uber guy calls me, I excuse myself from E, hurry down the stairs and into the car, smiling all the way. I like E and the gay hotel better and better.

The drive takes about fifteen minutes. I enter the grounds through a gateway and am immediately struck by the symmetrical beauty of the walkways, the channels of water, fountains, pools, expansive lawns. As I'd hoped, at this time of day there are only a few people here, walking and doing some morning exercising. I head for Humayun's tomb, which is located in the centre of the garden. It stands on a massive platform and resembles the Taj Mahal, except for its red sandstone, which is now glowing in the morning sun.

I begin to climb the steps up the twenty-feet-or-so-high platform. They are steep. I realise I am less well than I thought:

I start feeling weak and dizzy as I ascend, and for a moment imagine myself falling, hitting my head on the stone and dying. Eventually I reach the top. Parakeets flit about, bright green against the blue morning sky. I enter the large, octagonal chamber, and find it pleasantly cool. Through filigreed screens the morning sun illuminates the room. There are several tombs in here, of Humayun and his closest family members, I assume. Some doves are flying around, the clapping of their wings and their cooing echoing in the large chamber. Apart from that, nothing. Just me. And these graves. I close my eyes for a moment. I meditate on death, reflect that I too will die.

Once outside again, tired out, I sit down, leaning my back against a wall, close my eyes and enjoy the morning sun on my skin. Opening my eyes again, I take out my phone and google Humayun and his death.

The Mughal emperor had been busy in a meeting when he heard the call to prayer. A pious man, he rushed down some steps to get to the mosque, fell, fractured his skull and died. Rushing to Allah, I think to myself, and I take care as I make my way back down from the platform.

Outside the garden I find an auto-rickshaw. The auto-guy is having chai at a nearby tea stall. He signals to me to wait. While he finishes his drink I google breakfast places in the area. After a few minutes he comes over.

'Café Lota in the Crafts Museum, near Purana Qila,' I say.

'170,' he says.

'Nahin.'

'150.'

'To Uber behtar hai, yaar.'

'100.'

'Chalo.'

I get in, irritated. Every time you want to move a short distance in Delhi, this negotiation! And probably it is still overpriced. The auto-guy starts driving. Then he takes out a packet of cigarettes and offers me one; I decline, but appreciate the offer and immediately feel friendlier towards him. I am his first passenger of the day, I guess. I smile at him.

My phone vibrates and I take it out. I have received a message from a friend in Bombay, asking me how I am. I reply that I am well but I have caught a cold or something. He messages back, blaming the Delhi air. It started while I was still in Bombay, I tell him. And I tell him that Delhi has actually been pretty good to me so far.

At Café Lota I order French-pressed black coffee, and, because I can't decide between the two, I order both quinoa upma and mushroom uttapam. I start reading my book, but a conversation happening a few tables away is so loud I can't concentrate. I thought Delhiites were loud, but this guy is incredible! An American-Indian, I conclude from his accent. His friend is an Indian-Indian lady, I conclude from hers. The conversation is not even slightly interesting.

'I was offered something my hosts must have thought I'd like the other day, some greasy street food, but nobody in America eats this kind of stuff,' he complains. 'Americans are very health-conscious now. And the smoking here! Nobody smokes in America anymore.'

He moans on and on. Luckily they finish their meal – or more likely leave it – after ten minutes or so. A waiter clears their table. When he comes to clear mine, I order another coffee.

'Your coffee was excellent by the way. The quinoa upma and mushroom uttapam also. Sab kuch achcha tha, bahut achcha.' I say it softly, a whisper in Hindi to contrast with the American-Indian's arrogant English.

'Thank you, sir,' the waiter says and smiles.

I remain for a couple of hours, reading my book and making some notes. Then I order an Uber and head back to Greater Kailash.

I decide to visit M Block Market again. I pass a group of workers near a construction site. The mazdoor men, all in banians, are slim but ripped. They have dark, worker hands and arms and chests. Their tight jeans reveal the contours of their cocks and asses. I dawdle, feeling my cock grow. I want to watch them for as long as I can. Then some of them turn towards me, suspicious perhaps. I look away and pick up my pace.

I reach the small park in the middle of M Block Market. Someone is mowing the lawn. I stop and inhale the particular pleasant smell of freshly cut grass. At some distance from the guy mowing the lawn, I see two guys lying in the only spot where there is some shade, beneath a neem tree. One is sprawled on his back. The other lies on his side, facing his friend. He supports his head with one hand and puts his free hand casually on his friend's belly. Then he places one leg over the leg of his friend. I watch them for a while as they lie there entwined like that, seemingly oblivious, unselfconscious.

As I walk back to the hotel, stepping over the fallen palash flowers, I think about the massage offer.

'I was wondering, the massage, is it too late to order?' I ask E, who is in the lobby as usual.

'No, sir, it is possible,' he says, looking pleased I am ordering something from him for once.

'What kind of massage is it?' I ask, appreciating his white smile, full lips and chin dimple. 'And who does it?' For a moment I imagine – hope – that it is him.

'It's full-body and relax massage, sir. A professional will come. He will come to your room.'

'Okay. Let me think about it for a minute, and I'll let you know.'

I undress and lie down on the bed. I imagine E, his smile and chin dimple, his hands on me. I am lying on my back, a small piece of thin cloth barely covering my cock. He massages my shoulders, arms and chest, my legs and thighs, his hands moving closer to my crotch, the thin cloth, and my cock grows visibly, the cloth moves, and he smiles.

My phone sounds with a message. It is D. He asks about Humayun and what I am doing on my last evening in Delhi. I tell him I am considering having a massage. He suggests Mykonos, a gay spa which also has a nice rooftop café with a view of the Qutub Minar.

'That way you'd get both massage and minar,' he writes, followed by a crazy face. I google it. 'A rejuvenating experience.' 'Magnificent view of the Qutub.' 'An ideal place for men to meet men.' I order an Uber and have a quick shower.

On the way out I find E and tell him thanks but no thanks to the massage. He looks disappointed. I decide I will give him a generous tip tomorrow morning before leaving.

After spending what feels like forever in traffic, I spot the Qutub Minar in the distance, towering over the surrounding buildings and trees. A Hanuman temple was also mentioned as a landmark in the address of the spa. I look out for it, and soon I spot it as well.

'Here is good,' I tell the Uber guy.

I walk past the temple to a tall, modern building with a rainbow flag hanging outside it. I enter and take the stairs to the rooftop café. I walk over to the railing and look across the main road to the Qutub Minar. The soaring tower is surrounded by dense trees which make a green carpet below it. The evening sun makes the ancient structure of red sandstone and marble look soft and warm.

A guy comes up to me, young and lean, moustached, wearing black trousers with a shirt tucked in, elegantly and gentlemanly good-looking. Perhaps the manager or head waiter or something.

'What a view,' I say.

'Yeah, and the sun sets just near the Qutub. Would you like something to drink?'

'Could I have a fresh lime soda, salty?'

He nods. I have the place almost to myself, and I sit down on a comfortable sofa at the edge of the terrace facing the Qutub. The sun is on my face, intense but bearable. I look around and notice some cute boys in black T-shirts and jeans wandering between the tables; staff I think. They remind me of E and the boy in black kurta, but look more Nepali or Northeastern. I unbutton my shirt a bit so the sun caresses my neck and upper chest as well as my face. One of the boys brings me my drink. I sip it: cool, a little salty. I catch myself playing with the straw in my mouth, rolling it or rubbing my lips around it, biting into it a bit.

A ladybird lands in the dark soil of a potted plant. Red with black dots. I watch as it crawls up the green stem, then flits off into the sun's dazzle. I remember when I was little and I would put a ladybird on my hand and wish for something, and then it would fly away, sometimes leaving a small, yellow spot of pee on my hand. I smile.

By the time I finish my drink the sun feels cooler. I should go to the spa now, and then come back up to catch the sunset, I think to myself. I get the attention of one of the boys and pay for my drink.

I descend a couple of floors and stop at a door which says

'Spa'. I open it and enter a rather elegant reception area.

'Welcome,' says a pleasant receptionist, smartly dressed like the guy on the terrace, black trousers and shirt tucked in. I notice an information poster with the various offers and prices. The full spa package includes massage.

'Do you want the full package?' the receptionist asks.

'Yeah, I think so,' I say and give him two 500-rupees notes.

He gives me a 100-rupees note back. 'Come. I'll show you the guys.'

I follow him through into another room. Men are standing around or sitting on sofas in tight T-shirts and small sports shorts, medium to very physically attractive, all of them with a blank look. Most are young and look Nepali or Northeastern like the boys on the rooftop. One is different: older and taller, he has a beard and a small paunch. He reminds me a bit of XL guy. This is like a showroom, I think to myself. I feel anxious and hesitant. I have been to gay saunas before, but I have never paid for sex. I can just have a massage, I guess. I don't have to have sex. Actually I don't even know for certain that sex is being offered.

'So do they offer different kinds of massages?' I ask.

'No, it's all relax massage,' the receptionist says. 'You just choose one you like.'

'Okay,' I say. 'Maybe him,' I nod towards the older, taller guy.

He steps forward. 'Follow me,' he says. I do.

We enter a changing room. I am offered a white towel, sandals and a locker. I undress and put my clothes and things away. He waits at the door, watching me. Wearing only the towel around my waist and the sandals, I follow him along a corridor and down some steps. He walks fast. I hurry to keep up and arrive in a large, dimly-lit space that is almost like a darkroom. Perhaps it is.

'Where are you?' I ask.

'Here.'

My eyes adjust. Across from where I'm standing I see an open door with a sign next to it that says 'Massage'. I enter what turns out to be a small booth. He stands next to a massage table, shirtless already, unsmiling. This is routine for him, I guess.

'Lie down on your stomach,' he says blandly.

I remove the sandals and lie down. He starts massaging me, my toes, feet, calves. It is quiet. I feel uncomfortable. Sometimes I hear him sniffing. It sounds like he has a runny nose.

'You have a cold?' I ask, trying to make conversation.

'No,' he says. 'I went to a friend's house last night, and his mother had made rice with lots of chillies. That's why.' He speaks in a mix of Hindi and heavily North-Indian-accented English, and suddenly this feels more intimate and relaxed. He has a life outside this place, a friend, a friend with a mother, has eaten rice and chillies, too much, making his nose run.

'Now I should eat something sweet,' he says.

I smile. I find the idea that this would help him touching. I wonder if there is also a double entendre, that I am sweet and he wants to eat me.

He brings his hands higher up, up my legs, including my thighs in the massage. It feels good. I fall silent and let myself be massaged and enjoy it. He strokes me up and down the entire length of my legs now, all the way up my thighs, up to the towel, under the towel. His hands sometimes touch my ass cheeks. Now he even brushes lightly up against my hole. It makes me so horny, this teasing – if that is what it is. Perhaps nothing more will happen. Perhaps this is the best part anyway. Then, as he leans over me, moving his hands up the entire length of my legs, all the way up to my ass, I sense his shorts against my toes. I sense the soft textile and something harder underneath.

He moves round and comes up next to me, standing to my left, and starts massaging my lower back. My left hand is hanging just off the edge of the massage table. His shorts brush against my fingers. I am so turned on, not knowing what the boundaries are.

I make just the slightest movement with a finger or two, brush his hard cock with a fingertip, and then everything moves faster. He takes off his shorts, and I feel his naked cock against my fingers. I grab it without looking, small but rigid in my hand. Cut, I think. I feel his balls, surprisingly big. He climbs on top of me, pushes the towel further up so my ass is fully exposed, slides his cock between my ass cheeks, up against my hole.

'Do you have a condom?' he asks.

'No,' I say.

'Wait.'

He puts on his shorts again and leaves.

I am alone in the booth. Quiet. Waiting. The teasing, the not knowing, the uncertain boundaries, all of that was so exciting. Do we need to fuck? Do I even want to? But he has already gone out to get a condom. It would be awkward, even be rude perhaps, to say no now.

He comes back in. He takes off his shorts again.

'Can you suck, make me hard again?'

I smile and nod. I like that he asks me to do something for him too; that I can arouse him. I get off the table, kneel and put his small cock in my mouth. Quickly it swells and becomes hard again. He takes hold of my shoulders, raises me up, guides me back on the table, face down. He climbs on top and fucks me. I don't feel much, his cock being so small, but I make some noise, for his sake. After a few minutes he pulls out and takes off the condom.

'Suck me more?'

He gets me up from the table, onto the floor and sits down on the table himself. I suck his cock. He comes in my mouth, doesn't pull out, and I taste and swallow it.

'Chillies,' I say, look up at him and smile.

'Now hand job,' he says, jumps off the table and gets me back onto the table, on my back this time.

'I want you to come, so you're done, so no one else will have you,' he says.

Is it professional pride? Is it competiveness? Is he a bit jealous and possessive?

In any case he is doing a great job, his hands on my cock. It doesn't take long till I come. He gives me some paper from a roll, and I clean myself up.

'There,' he says, pointing to a small rubbish bin. There is already some wadded-up paper in it, and I think of how many others he must have had sex with in here. He pulls on his shorts. I wrap the towel around my hips.

'So how long have you worked here?' I ask him.

'Two years. Since I came to Delhi,' he says.

'And how many massages a day?'

'Three or four,' he says. 'But I don't always bring the client to discharge.'

'Oh. Okay.'

'I liked you,' he says.

I smile.

'Do you live here?' he continues.

'No. Just visiting.'

Suddenly it becomes black and silent around us, a power outage. We both sit on the massage table in the windowless room. The table provides us with something stable. We sit close to each other, the outer sides of our arms touching in the black silence. It probably doesn't even last a full minute, but when the electricity is back – the sound of a machine starting up somewhere, lights back on – it feels like we have shared something special; that an important transformation has taken place, and we see each other differently.

'You're very beautiful,' he says, letting his eyes wander over me.

'Thanks. You too,' I say.

'What's your name?' he asks me.

I tell him my name, a Hindu name. He tells me his, a Muslim name. Let us call him H here.

'How long are you in Delhi?' he asks.

'I leave tomorrow morning,' I say.

'When are you back?' he asks.

'I don't know,' I say.

'Oh,' he says. 'I'll miss you.'

'Do you have a boyfriend?' I ask.

'No,' he says.

'Would you like one?'

'Yeah,' he says, pauses, and then continues, 'Our salary is very low. But sometimes we get a tip.'

'I'll tip you,' I say.

We go back to the locker room. I find a 100-rupees note and give it to him.

'Let's go upstairs and have a beer and some food,' he says.

Is he asking because he wants to hang out with me or because he wants me to buy him food and drinks?

'Not now,' I say. 'I want to use the spa a little bit more.

Thank you for the massage!'

He looks sad. I feel bad and leave him. I go to another room, a steam bath. Weak red lights vaguely contour the several men sitting and standing there. I sit down on a bench. Someone touches my arm. I find a thigh that I touch. After a minute or so I take my hand back and leave the steam bath. I go through to the joint showers. A glass wall separates the booths from each other. I see a white guy with a shaved head and an Indian guy in the booth next to mine. Is it the white guy from my hotel? They are touching each other. The white guy sees me looking, invites me round with a wave. I go in. We kiss. I touch their cocks and balls; they touch mine. The white guy fingers me. I smile at them and leave again. I keep hoping for something but realise that these fleeting sexual encounters only bore me now.

One part of the spa area is only shielded from outside view by some wooden panels and a lattice fence. Through the gaps I can see people passing by. I hear sounds, evening sounds, bells from the Hanuman temple, boisterous birds settling in trees, children playing. It makes me think of childhood and home. I remain there, with the thin divide between us, longing. I remember the sense of belonging and community at the dargahs the evening before. I go back to the locker, put on my clothes and leave the spa.

I climb up to the rooftop café again. It is more crowded now. On the sofa where I was sitting earlier are a man and a woman, a romantic couple it seems. I sit down by myself at a table nearby. I wonder if some people just come for the food and drinks and view. Perhaps they don't even know this is a queer venue. I rest my eyes on the Qutub Minar and the sun setting beside it. It is beautiful. I enjoy it. And I enjoy being part of the mixed crowd, all of us here for the sunset. Then I think of H, downstairs in the spa, in the never fully lit rooms, and of him asking me to come up here with him, and I feel a knot tighten in my stomach.

Once the sun is down I order an Uber. I keep getting messages that it is delayed. Apparently there is a lot of traffic. Some of the cute boys are putting candles on the tables now. I order a tulsi tea from one of them. Some people can't praise tulsi enough. Perhaps it will make me feel better. I think of how I just swallowed H's sperm, a sex worker's sperm. Can I get an STD from that? Soon after my tulsi tea arrives I get a message that my Uber is only five minutes away. I blow on the hot tea and take some sips. When the app tells me it is one minute away, I pay and leave. On the way down the stairs I bump into H on his way up.

'Let's go up,' he says.

'Sorry. I have to go now.'

'Just one minute.' He takes my hand. 'Please.'

I let him lead me up to the rooftop terrace café again. Then I let go of his hand.

'It's nice, na,' he says.

'Yeah.'

He takes my hand again. 'Come back on Friday.'

'I'm leaving early tomorrow morning.'

My phone rings.

'I'm outside the Hanuman temple.' It is the Uber guy.

'Yes, I'm coming,' I say. 'Sorry.'

I let go off H's hand again. 'I have to go now. Sorry.'

I hurry down the stairs.

While being driven away I think about how his sperm is inside my body, and I find that somehow ameliorating, the departure less brutal because of that.

I

I wake up the next morning to a message from D, asking me about the massage and minar. I think about H. I think about his sperm, the way in which some of it, some of him, has been absorbed and become a part of me by now.

'Good morning, sir.' E greets me in the lobby. 'Breakfast?'

'That would be nice, but I have to leave very soon.'

'No problem. I can prepare it quickly.'

'Okay. Thank you.' I smile. E smiles his nice smile back. I sit down at the big dining table, and he serves me. I taste chillies in the anda bhurji. I like it. I drink some sweet chai. I like that too.

'This is for you,' I say and hand E some 100-rupees notes. 'Thank you for everything.'

'Thank you, sir. Please come back.'

The Uber guy calls. E insists on carrying my small suitcase and comes down with me. I get in the car, and he closes the door on me and waves me goodbye.

From the back seat of the car I glimpse the palash trees, their fiery red flowers, and I hear the call to morning prayer, long a, liquid l.

I will miss Delhi.

Sunset Point

'Puja, I love you!' It sounded like a young man's voice. Though we were getting close to Echo Point I didn't hear an echo.

Veer and I were in Matheran, on our last trip together before I left the country. In a slightly mocking tone I repeated it to him – *'Puja, I love you!'* – and laughed a little. Immediately I regretted it.

'Do you want to go there,' I asked, 'Echo Point?'

'Do you?'

'I'd rather go straight to Sunset Point.'

We passed the sign for Echo Point and kept on going, alone on the path enveloped by a dense forest of mango, peepal, banyan, climbers, ferns, moss. Apart from the increasingly distant, joyful shouts and reverberations coming from Echo Point, we were surrounded only by the constant chorus of cicadas.

'Amazing the sound these little things manage to make,' I said.

'Amazing,' he agreed. 'They have a sort of musical organ inbuilt. Timbal I think they're called, like the Brazilian drums. Membranes vibrate rapidly, and the almost hollow abdomen works as a resonance chamber amplifying the sound. They do it to attract mates.'

'Naturally.' I smiled, and Veer looked at me, his face a question mark. 'To attract mates,' I added, and he smiled and kissed me quickly on my cheek.

'There is also a distinct distress call that some species make, a broken and erratic sound,' he continued.

'The things you know,' I said.

'Sorry, Ram. I'm a bit of a nerd.'

'You know I like that,' I said.

'There are also courtship songs, generally quieter,' he continued, 'after a mate has been drawn in by the calling song.'

A Bollywood song, a current hit, increased in volume behind us. I turned and saw some youngsters talking and laughing while walking along the forest path. One was holding up his mobile phone with its loudspeaker on.

'Why the fuck do these people come to the forest and mountains if they just want the noise of the city?' I said.

Veer agreed, rolling his eyes and shaking his head.

'Let's go slowly and let them pass us,' I suggested.

We slowed to a dawdle. As I watched the teenage boys and girls go by, I softened a little. Their idea of the forest, of a day out, of being together, of love, of joy, was informed by boisterous Bollywood films, I told myself. I even had some warm feelings for them as with their song and smiles they disappeared among the trees ahead of us.

'Already I'm feeling more relaxed.'

'Yeah. This trip is so beautiful. Thank you,' Veer said.

'Thank you,' I said.

'For what? You paid for everything.'

'For coming. The experience is created jointly.'

I wanted us to be equals. But, really, we weren't. I was leaving the country, and he was staying. Maybe that was why I had insisted on paying for this whole trip.

Out of the corners of my eyes I was looking at his feet on the brownish-red Matheran soil of the path. I heard the soft sound of his steps. I wondered if it was okay to fall into an easy silence; just to be and enjoy. I wanted that, and for some scattered seconds my mind felt quieter. But mostly this was just another kind of outward silence, one that provided only a thin cover for inner tension.

'Let's have a gin and tonic when we get back to the hotel,' I suggested. 'We can have it on that beautiful veranda before dinner.'

'Yeah, like that first time, when we met at Salvation Star.' He smiled.

'Mm,' I said.

I was so attracted to him then – more than he was to me, I remembered fearing. I wondered what he was thinking now. Perhaps he was worrying that whatever it was between us was coming to an end with me leaving the country. In response to my constant need to clarify that I couldn't commit to anything for the future, he would say that he was fine with that – 'Let's just enjoy the present' – but at other times he would say, 'Just put me in your suitcase, na?' He would say it with a smile, giving me the space to laugh and not have to take him seriously, knowing that if I felt trapped he might lose me altogether.

In the midst of the shimmering cicada noise I suddenly heard the call of a single bird. It sang, was silent for a few seconds, then sang again. I didn't recognise it.

'Do you know what bird that was?' I asked.

Veer shook his head no.

I whistled a tune, trying to engage it. But the bird gave no response. I whistled again.

'I think you scared it away, Ram.'

'Oh no.' I felt bad; he was probably right.

We walked in silence again. The forest path curved gently uphill.

'Do you know the story of Echo?' I said.

'No.'

'She was in love with Narcissus, and,' I said, 'I think I better google it so I tell it correctly. I'll look it up later if you want.'

'Okay.'

We dawdled to a halt in front of an abandoned Parsi mansion with a stone and iron gate, almost reclaimed by the forest now. I felt a childlike desire to sneak in and explore it.

'Shall we go in?' I asked.

'No, someone may own it,' he said.

'Okay.'

We walked on in silence again. Then – perhaps for us to do something together; if not trespassing, then at least this – he took my hand, squeezed it, and without looking at me, without waiting for me to reciprocate or promise something back, he walked faster, almost breaking into a run, still holding onto my hand, so I ran with him, and we laughed. It felt simple and innocent, like we were children running through the forest. But it also felt like we had little time left.

It was four p.m. when we got to Sunset Point, still a couple of hours until sunset. We left the forest behind and emerged onto a flat, open space patched with worn, brown grass. At the far end, near the cliff-edge, was a small shop, bright blue, proudly declaring itself the 'Sunset Vadapav Centar' in red capital letters.

'I need something small to eat. Do you want anything?' Veer asked.

'No, thanks. I'll just wait here,' I said and sat down under a massive mango tree.

I watched him walk over to the shop. Behind me, on the other side of the tree, I heard some Gujjus, men, women and children. A family. They were sharing a meal. It reminded me of my own family and outings when I was little, and I felt a little nostalgic. Veer came back with a vada pav and a Bisleri. He handed me the bottle.

'Thanks,' I said and drank of the cool mineral water.

He sat down opposite me. Seeing his vada pav, some macaque monkeys came scurrying down from the trees and gathered around us.

'I read something earlier from an old guidebook, *Hill of Beauty*,' I said. 'There was a section on the monkeys of Matheran. They are the biggest rascals. Familiarity has made them contemptuous of humans and they have learnt one or two human tricks. Something along those lines.'

Veer ate his vada pav with both hands; the monkeys remained at a distance.

On the stretch of worn grass the Gujju children were now playing some version of tag, running around, shouting cheerfully.

'I'd like children one day,' Veer said.

A few days ago I had told him that my ex and I had been on the verge of adopting a girl, but then he had an affair and we split up.

'I think it takes a lot of energy though,' I said.

'Yeah. I couldn't do it alone.'

Having finished his food, Veer lay down with his head on my lap.

'Shall I read you the story of Echo now?' I asked.

'Sure.'

I googled 'Echo' and 'Greek myth', and paraphrased from a site: 'Zeus had started spending a lot of time down on Earth. So eventually his wife Hera became suspicious, thinking he might be having affairs, and came looking for him. Echo, trying to cover for Zeus, distracted her by lengthy chatter. When Hera realised what was going on she cursed Echo. From then on she would only be able to repeat the last words said to her.'

'Hera, the bitch,' Veer said.

'Well, it can't have been easy for her, I guess. Zeus was very promiscuous. If I'd been married to him, I'd have killed him,' I said, slightly shocked by my own choice of words, the violence of them.

I remembered how, as we were leaving Salvation Star the first time we met, he had said something about a guy who walked past us, 'hot' or something. Then he had asked why I became so silent. 'I want a lover to be focused on me,' I said, 'not talk to me about others he might find attractive.'

'Anyway,' I said, 'later in life Echo noticed Narcissus while the young man was out hunting with his friends. She followed him quietly, longing for him, but because of the curse she was unable to call out to him. Narcissus got separated from his friends and shouted, "Is anyone there?" Echo repeated his words, "Is anyone there?" Startled, Narcissus answered her, "Come here." Echo rushed to him. But Narcissus, seeing Echo coming towards him, ready to throw her arms around him, was appalled and rejected her. Still, much later, when he was dying, she mourned him. Looking at himself in the mirror of a pond, Narcissus said, "I loved you in vain. Farewell." Echo responded, "Farewell." With time she also began to waste away. Today all that remains are her bones turned to stone and the sound of her voice.'

I put my phone away. I felt the weight of Veer's head light on my lap. I looked at him, his eyes closed. 'Darling?' I said.

'Beautiful,' he said and put a hand on my leg. 'And sad.'

'Yeah,' I said.

'Let's just rest here, waiting for the sunset,' he said.

I rested my head against the mango tree. We had left Bombay early in the morning. Now we could just relax and do nothing.

After an hour or so the ground and the tree-trunk began to

feel hard and lumpy, so we got up. More people had gathered by then, families, groups of friends, young and old lovers. And along with the people came more monkeys.

We walked out to the furthest point, beyond the crowd of people. Veer went ahead of me. He wanted to sit all the way out on the precipice.

'Come,' he said.

'I don't know.'

'Come. It's okay,' he insisted.

I went over to him, and we sat there together at the edge, a panoramic view of the ghats and valleys before us. We watched the sun become a flaming red ball resting on the horizon. Then, slowly yet also somehow suddenly, the sky darkened, everything softened. I felt a slight breeze and exhaled.

We got up, left the point and, after passing through the now quiet and still-sitting crowd, started walking back through the forest. The red soil path almost glowed in the dusk. I heard no cicadas now.

'I really hope they have gin and tonic,' Veer said.

'Yeah.'

Then I heard the bird again.

'Did you hear that bird again?' I asked.

'Yeah,' Veer said. 'Now don't scare it away.'

'I won't,' I said.

J.

'Your cousin brother J, he never married, did he?' I asked.

'No.'

'And he got very depressed?'

'I think that's why he never married,' my mother said. 'Have another waffle, Ram. Have one with brunost. You like that.'

'Thanks, but I'm really full now, mamma. So J was a lot older than you?'

'Oh yes, Ram. Let me see. I was still a child when he went to Bombay to study, so he was much older than me.'

'He was a doctor, right? Where did he work again?'

'Yeah. It was in the villages near the farm.'

'Mm.'

'He was very well liked. He was very kind.'

'You don't know why he got so depressed?'

'No.' Silence. 'I wondered if it was heartbreak.' She almost laughs, or maybe it is more a sigh.

'Mm.'

'But I don't really know that. Maybe he couldn't marry the one he wanted, or... I don't know. And then he stopped working.'

'He quit his job?'

'Yeah. It wasn't safe to continue. I can understand that: as a doctor you have to be quite focused, you know.'

'He lived by himself or what?'

'No, no, he lived with his brother and his brother's family. They all lived on the farm. And then when he died, well, all his money – it was millions – went to his nephew who now lives in America, you know.'

'But it wasn't talked about, the fact that he never married?'

'Oh yes. Everybody wanted him to get married. Ba was really concerned. "What a sad life," she used to say to his mother. "What will he do when he gets older?"'

'Mm.'

'Ba always used to say that.'

'And what did they respond, his family?'

'I don't know. He had to make an effort himself also, I guess.'

'So he didn't want to or what?'

'I don't know.'

'Hm. You don't think he was gay?'

'No.'

'You don't think so?'

'No, not at all. No, I don't think so, Ram.'

'Why not?'

'Because I know, don't I?'

'Hm.'

'I know he wasn't.' Silence. 'You know, I didn't know much about gay and all that before.'

'No.'

'It's really strange. I've never really thought about that.'

'That he might have been?'

'Yeah.'

'I just thought since he never married and got so depressed and all that.'

'Mm. I don't really know. We could ask Moti Ben, but I don't think...'

'People didn't talk about things like that then?'

'No, no, no, no.' She laughs a little, then stops. 'But it's entirely possible that he was.'

'It must have been very difficult.'

'Mm.'

Silence. A long silence. The sound of a clock ticking.

'What are you thinking, mamma?'

'Now I'm thinking about what you said, what you asked. I don't know, Ram. It's so strange to think about.' Silence. 'And then I'm thinking about how it is here, now. People like to think it's so open and accepting, but it isn't always. You know, there are two men who live just around the corner.'

'Partners?'

'Yeah, partners.'

'Yeah.'

'And they have been partners for so many years. And now they are older; one is a senior citizen. And we are friends, not because of you or anything, I just like them.'

'Yeah.'

'They used to have a dog. You know, one of those dogs with the long ears. So cute!'

We both chuckle. 'Well, one day the dog came up to me when I was out walking. That's how I got to know them. But the last time I saw them, they had lost him. He was very old, you know.' She clears her throat. 'Paul makes jokes about them. But he makes fun of everyone. And Anna talks about them, but face-to-face with them she acts so nice it makes me sick. In a way everyone...' She takes a breath, strained. 'It's what I told you: that life, the way you lead your life, it will be tough.'

'Mm.'

'Because it's one of the weak groups, isn't it? Even here it's still like that. And people do, they always pick on those they are allowed to pick on.'

'But things have changed a lot, at least where I live in Oslo, mamma. I'm okay, you know. You don't have to worry about me.'

'Yeah. I really hope so.'

'Even in India these things are changing now, you know. But it must have been very difficult in the past.'

'It was very, very difficult.'

'When you couldn't even talk about it.'

'I had never even heard about it, Ram.'

'No.'

'Think about that.'

'Because there were people in those days too.'

'Yes, absolutely. Think about that.'

'And many probably felt alone and depressed.'

'Mm.' Silence. 'I really hope you find someone soon, Ram. I want to die knowing you're happy.'

'I'm okay, mamma. I really am. Don't worry. And you're not

dying yet.'

'Did you meet someone in India?'

'Yeah. But I don't know if it will continue.'

'It's far. Maybe it's better to find someone in Oslo, where you live?'

'Maybe.'

Silence.

'Tell me the story about how you first came to Norway and met Pappa again.'

'Oh, Ram.' She laughs.

A Safe Harbour

'Break,' he says at some point during the conversation, and something breaks all right. It probably started a while ago, but now it feels like I am free falling.

*

'The breath is your anchor,' says an annoying American voice on my mindfulness app. 'And a safe harbour you can always return to.' Fuck, I think to myself, I also need another's body as a harbour. I start creating a profile on Grindr, then delete it. I call good friends and family instead. They meet me and they hold me, either physically or otherwise, through their presence; often both.

*

It is a hot, dry Delhi summer. Normally we would have escaped together to the mountains or somewhere else more bearable. Now I am alone in this massive house in South Delhi, a property I inherited, but which we moved into together, and created a home in together. He has packed most of his stuff and left. I am still surrounded by everything we bought together, the Rajasthani teak table from a trip to Jodhpur, the Gond painting of a tree full of birds. And there are constant ambushes; memories hide behind the most everyday actions and objects. I am shaving in front of the bathroom mirror one morning, not quite awake, when I suddenly think of him and lose my breath. It's the razor. We were on holiday in Goa together. I don't remember what I said, what he said, I only remember that it was nice, we had a nice time together on the beach. And then, back at the hotel before going out for dinner, he suggested that I let him shave me, the blade sharp on my skin, on my face and neck, his concentrating gaze, his hands tenderly cradling me.

*

Sometimes I reflect on what went wrong. Sometimes I get too caught up in these thoughts and memories. Sometimes I become aware of my breath and my body, let the emotions move through me, let the memories come and go. Sometimes I am able to wish myself well, and to wish him well.

*

But I also need another man's body. I need to be held. I need the certain confirmation of another man's erection. I create a profile, bare upper body, partially hidden face. Soon I see another naked upper body and partially hidden face, 250 feet away, athletic, 5 feet 8 inches tall, XL, top.

'Hi,' I write.

'Hi,' he responds.

'Some more photos?' I ask and get a face pic. Fair skin, blue eyes, dense hair, trimmed beard.

'Handsome! And there's something familiar about you,' I continue, and send a face pic in return.

'Why, it's the sexy neighbour!' he replies with a wink.

'That's right! You're just across the street, no? I guess we've never really met properly. Maybe we should do that some day?'

'I'd love to. But don't you have a partner? Open relationship?'

'Break.'

'Oh.'

'Or end.'

'I'm sorry.'

'Thanks, but let's not talk so much about that now.'

'Okay.'

'So, XL?' I write and wink and soon get another photo: a Gillette shaving foam can and a cock to compare, thick, probably eight or nine inches long, cut.

'Impressive,' I continue, heart beating and horny, but also a little scared after seeing the size of his cock.

'Thanks! I'm Aziz by the way.'

'I'm Virat. Want to meet now?' I ask.

'Sure.'

I jump in the shower and prepare myself for the possibility of sex, and thinking that we might have sex makes me hard. I put on sports shorts, a T-shirt and sandals, and leave the house.

Outside the summer night is still so hot that I almost break into a sweat just crossing the street. On the other side I tell a watchman who I am visiting, and he directs me to a lift.

Aziz opens the door to his flat wearing denim shorts and a simple white T-shirt. Neither T-shirt nor shorts are tight, but his chest, arms, thighs and crotch fill them amply, almost spilling out.

He shows me around his flat. It's spacious. A Kashmiri rug decorates the living room floor like an enormous piece of jewellery, sapphire blue, ruby red, emerald green. I look out of his living room window, and down there it is, only partially hidden by the purple-blue jacaranda: our house.

'You can almost see into our living room,' I say. And it feels strange to look down on it from here, and I just said our, and he knows that I have been a we until only recently.

'Yes.'

'So do you, Aziz?' I ask with a smile, and when I say Aziz I become more aware of him, of us, here and now.

'It's happened,' he says and moves closer with his blue eyes and bright white smile, and for a moment I imagine Kashmir's white mountains and piercing blue sky. He is taller than me, and when he presses against me I feel the head of his rigid cock against my stomach; I am reminded of the photo, the Gillette can, and I get hornier but also a little scared again. He cradles my face in his large hands, bends his head and kisses me on the mouth; I close my eyes and slip my arms around his neck. His hands move down to my hips, he guides me backwards, lays me down on a sofa and climbs on top of me. I open my eyes. He looks at me, his expression almost serious.

'Beautiful,' he says, and I look to the side a little, smile and kiss him again. His tongue is in my mouth; his erection grows bigger and bigger against mine; I lift my legs and wrap them around him, a small sound escaping from my mouth.

'Do you want to fuck?' he whispers in my ear.

'I think so. You?'

'I've wanted to fuck you for a long time,' he says, looking me in the eyes, and while he holds my gaze he lifts me up. For a moment he stands like that, holding me, my legs wrapped around his hips, my arms around his neck; I am carried like that. Then, carefully, we both let go and I come down, setting my feet on the Kashmiri rug.

He takes my hand and leads me into a dimly lit bedroom. The furnishings are simple; the bed is large. The room is pleasantly cool.

'Only if you want.'

'I do,' I say.

He smiles and pulls my T-shirt up and over my head. He strokes my chest and arms, his hands warm on me in the air-conditioned room, and it feels as if he is sculpting me, creating my body here and now. I pull off his T-shirt. I explore his muscles, skin and chest hair, thinking how afterwards it would be nice to rest my head on his chest, sleep there for the night maybe.

He slides one hand down the back of my shorts and grabs one ass cheek, holds my face with the other. I moan, and he kisses me. He pulls my shorts down, grabs an ass cheek in each hand, pulls me closer, and through the fabric of his shorts I feel his erection against my now naked body. I want to see, so I create some space between us. Looking down at the contours of his cock through his shorts, thick and long along one side, I imagine the denim almost bursting. I unbutton him, and out it springs, hard and soft at the same time, warm, pulsating, powerful. I kneel, a bedroom rug comfortable under my knees, look up at him and smile. I lick around the head, let my tongue slide up and down the shaft; I get the head and then some of the shaft into my mouth, and he groans. After a while he bends down, holds me by my shoulders, and I get up to a kiss. He lays me down on the bed, on my back, looks at me, all of me, naked on the bed.

'You're so hot,' he says and shakes his head as if in disbelief.

His words and gaze and erection remove every shred of shame and uncertainty I feel about my body. It fills me with joy, that I turn him on so much.

He walks over to a drawer, his swinging erection somehow huge in the room, and finds a condom and lube. Lying down next to me, he squirts a little lube onto his forefinger and places it against my hole, cool and moist, pushes gently so I open a bit, and while his tongue enters my mouth, I feel his finger slide further into me.

'Okay?'

'Yeah,' I say, smiling back.

He places a pillow under my hips and I spread my legs. He slides the finger in again, then another finger, two fingers side by side, preparing me. Then he takes hold of his cock, rolls on the condom, and I feel the smoothly bulging head against my hole. This will never work, I think to myself, but he takes his time, bumping his cock teasingly against the entrance, rubbing it back and forth, and I relax more; I want to have him; I want to open for him, this familiar stranger. I wrap my legs around him. Then the head is inside. I grunt; he stays there, looks at me; I am biting my lower lip.

'Still okay?'

'Yes.'

'Does it hurt?'

'Not too much.'

'No more?'

'More,' I say, laughing a little, my hole relaxing and dilating as I do.

'Okay,' he says and smiles. I look again into those blue eyes and I feel him filling me.

'Can you just stay inside me for a little while?' I ask, and he does. He fills me up completely, lies on top of me, a welcome weight, and kisses me gently on the nose and forehead.

'This is so good,' he says, 'to be inside you.'

Slowly he begins to move back and forth, then faster. I place his forearm against my mouth so I won't make too much noise, and to better endure the pain and pleasure.

'Break,' he says with a smile, and pulls out, making me gasp. 'I want this to last.'

He lies down beside me and strokes a couple of fingers

down my chest and my stomach. He spits in his hand, grabs my cock and moves his hand on it. Then he turns me onto my stomach and kisses my neck. He climbs on top of me, straddling my waist so his still huge cock slides along the groove of my lower back. He stretches for the lube, and soon I feel the coolness again, and then once more his cock inside me, this time from behind. After a while he positions me so I am on all fours. He grabs hold of my cock with one of his hands. I hear him breathe, and I too breathe faster. He fills me up again and again, thrusting movements and then tremors; he groans with pleasure, and I too come in spasms. He pulls out slowly, hugs me and places lots of little kisses on my shoulders and neck.

'That was fucking insane,' he says. 'Just wait here. I'll get a towel.'

'Okay.'

I could hardly move right now in any case: my legs are trembling, my head is spinning. He leaves the room and returns with a hand towel. He strokes the slightly damp towel over my stomach, my crotch and on the bed-sheet where I came.

Suddenly there is a crack of thunder. I look round at the bedroom window, which is covered by blackout curtains. Outside the city must be caught in another summer storm.

'Stay the night?' he asks.

I smile and nod.

'And if I get really horny do I have your permission to fuck you again later during the night?'

'Sure.'

He lies on his back, and I rest my head on his chest. I hear his heart beating and the AC humming, steady, comforting sounds.

'So, Virat, are you a coffee or chai person?'

'Coffee.'

During the night I sense that he is about to enter me again and half wake up. I gladly let him fuck me for a few minutes. After he has come I fall into a deeper sleep, and then: 'Good morning, handsome.'

Aziz is standing at the side of the bed with two cups, naked in all his glory and completely at ease. There is the smell of fresh black coffee. I smile and sit up; he hands me a cup and climbs in beside me. Through the window – he must have opened the curtains earlier – I see a golden shower: an amaltas tree in full bloom, one of the few but gorgeous gifts Delhi can offer in summer.

'This is so good,' I say as I sip the coffee. 'The coffee and everything.'

'I'm glad,' he says, smiling, 'and one day I'll make you Kashmiri kahwa.'

*

Aziz and I continue to meet. But this won't last. One evening, towards the end of the summer, he says he has started falling for me, and that it is probably a mistake since I am just coming out of a long relationship and will need time to adjust. I nod. I say something. Then we embrace one last time before I go home and lie down on my own bed for the night.

The next morning I go to the bathroom to shave. I take the razor and shaving foam out of the cabinet. And when I squeeze the nozzle so a little foam comes out, I smile. Gillette. I wet my face and apply some of the cool, airy foam. I shave and see another face appear in the mirror. I hear the water running, and I exhale. The next breath I follow all the way out.

TGV to Geneva

I am sitting by the window, facing what we leave behind rather than in the direction of travel. I am listening to Sam Smith's 'Stay With Me'. It is that summer. Can I listen to it without thinking about my ex and our recent break-up; without starting to cry in public? I take off the headphones and look around me.

An older gentleman in a beige suit sits on the other side of the aisle, facing forward. He takes out an iPhone and snaps a few photos of the view. Green-sided mountains, blue sky, white clouds, light in movement. I think about the acronym NSA, and its Grindr meaning, which I only recently learnt: No Strings Attached.

A woman in a purple skirt and carefully-applied make-up sits diagonally across from me. She has a mischievous smile. Using her feet, she slips off some sandals and provocatively puts her bare feet on the empty seat by the aisle, effectively fencing me in.

A young man enters the carriage, says 'excusez-moi' to the purple lady. She moves her legs out of the way and he sits down next to her, by the window, directly opposite me. I pull my legs back a little so our knees don't clash. He is French-looking. Slim, well-groomed, glasses, summer blond beard, a shirt that is rolled up to reveal summer blond arms, some veins visible on their paler inner sides, open at the neck, a little hair on his chest. He takes out a book – Zola, so French – puts it on the table between us, leans a little forward, opens it and reads.

I am tired and sink down in the seat. Can I stretch out one leg? I try it, don't bump him, so am probably slightly to one side of, or in between, his legs. I am about to fall asleep. And then contact, a light touch against one side of my leg, then both. I am in between. Merely a momentary touch, but the sensation lingers. I open my eyes, meet his, bleu, the purple lady sleeps, pulsating penis, la bite. Under the table, the three of us in this moment, and no one to see. Massive mountains meet clouds. He is wearing shorts. His hands move to his thighs, straightening them. Our gazes meet, my heart hammering, Zola on the table, train rolling along the tracks. He leans back, closes his eyes. Winks at me? I put on my headphones, 'You Wish' by Nightmares on Wax, close my eyes, sense from the inside that I am smiling. I let myself sink into the chair, one knee slid forward; it must be near his crotch now. Knee falls out to the side, against the inside of his thigh, a warmth, and then a hand.

I wake to see a man in a black T-shirt across from me, clean-shaven, other eyes, and the purple lady smiles at me.

CockTail D'Amore

It is 3 p.m. on a Sunday, and I am near the back of a queue to enter a nightclub. 'Nightclub' may not be the right word, I guess: CockTail d'Amore is a weekend-long party, one of Berlin's top queer parties allegedly. I text the sexy gay couple from KitKatClub who told me to come, saying, 'I'm here but there is quite a queue.' One of them texts back, 'Great! The music and mood is good, the guys are hot, and we have some enhancers for you once you're in.'

On my left are some green trees and shrubs. On my right is a wall covered in street art. The building – possibly an abandoned factory – looks derelict. Barbed wire surrounds an outside clubbing area. Music pounds from within.

In front of me are two guys speaking Hebrew, Israelis I guess. One is small with a moustache, in a sleeveless shirt and rough denim shorts that are slightly sagging. The other is wearing glasses, nicer trousers and a shirt. Behind me I hear German and a Slavic language, Russian I think.

We are not moving. This may take time. But I can always meditate. I practice being here and now, loving awareness.

I breathe in.

I breathe out.

I focus on the young Israeli with the moustache. May you be held by loving presence. May you be filled with loving presence. I focus on his companion with glasses. May you be held by loving presence. May you be filled with loving presence. Looking down, I notice an ant by my foot. Arching its tiny neck, it seems to be bathing in a splash of sunlight. Someone walks past, their vast feet close to the ant. How risky that little life in the light. May you be held by loving presence. May you be filled with loving. A shoe comes down. As it lifts I notice that the small movements of the ant have ceased. Dead now.

We shuffle two-three steps forward. Now I sense a warmth on my neck, the sun shining through leaves. I look round. The leaves are trembling as if tickled by the light. Some of the movement and light is transported to my face, and I smile.

Perhaps because of this the Israeli guy with glasses says, 'At least there is sun while we're waiting.'

'Yeah,' I smile at him.

'First time here?'

I nod.

'I'm David – and this is Aron.'

'Hi. I'm Vihaan.'

'Anyway, it's worth the wait,' David says.

'So I've heard,' I say, 'I'm meeting some people inside.'

'Are you visiting?'

'Yeah. I just arrived this Friday, from India. A good friend of mine lives here now.'

'The guy you're meeting inside?'

'No. He stayed home. We already had a long night clubbing.'

'Berlin is the right place for that.'

'And you live here?'

'Yeah, at least for a while. I've been taking some time off, just reading and clubbing. I'm in between things back home – Israel.' Perhaps he has just finished military service. 'Excuse me, Vihaan, I need to go take a piss. On the way back I'll find a shop and buy us something to drink while queueing. Do you want beer or anything else?'

'I'm good, thanks,' I say.

'You, I know,' he says to Aron and leaves.

Aron looks at me, our eyes meet, and we smile briefly.

'So what have you done so far on your visit?' Aron asks.

'Yesterday we went to Sachsenhausen.'

'Oh. I haven't been myself yet. I should at some point, I guess. I have some family members who died there.'

'I'm so sorry.'

'Yeah. They were Jewish. We are Jewish, I guess.'

I nod.

'So where did you go clubbing last night?' he asks.

'KitKat.'

'What did you think? Anything like that in India?'

'Not that I know. I liked it, the freedom and diversity, the sex-positive environment.'

I remember the couple I saw on the sofa as I first entered there with my friend: a corporate-looking guy in a well-cut suit fingering a woman wearing only a black bra and high heels. I remember an old, bald man standing naked in a corner watching people and jerking off. I remember the guy in a wheelchair and the older dominatrix in leather who had him on a leash. And I remember the sexy gay couple in jockstraps looking at me and touching themselves and each other.

I went to the dancefloor with my friend. Soon the sexy gay couple found me there, and we started touching and kissing. They offered me a pill, which I took. One of them slipped his hand inside my briefs, between the cheeks, the other took my hand and placed it on his cock, which was semi-hard and barely contained by the jockstrap. Did I want to fuck? Maybe. But not there. They suggested we exchange numbers and leave the place together later and go to their place. After that they disappeared. I danced with my friend. And then another guy came up to me. We danced close. I noticed the couple from before with another guy on the dancefloor, kissing and fondling him. This free movement of people, without jealousy, was liberating.

'But I don't know, after a while at KitKat I also felt somewhat sad, something I can't quite put my finger on,' I say to Aron.

Perhaps it was partly an effect of the after all unknown pill the couple had offered me and I had taken. Perhaps it was jetlag. Perhaps it was a sudden rush of loneliness on the cramped dancefloor. Perhaps it was a sense of the superficiality and fleetingness of the interactions around me. Perhaps it was the whisper of spirit that was almost completely drowned out by the loud music and lights. Perhaps it was the visit to Sachsenhausen earlier that day. I had learnt that gay men and other deviants were also among the victims at the concentration camp. Now on the dancefloor I felt that everyone here was only concerned with random sex; and I was surprised by a sad, furious voice in my head that blared: Just gas us then!

'I can recognise that, I think,' Aron says.

I nod. 'You live here?'

'I guess so. I've been here for a year. I'm working in a café now.'

'What's it called? Any good? I love breakfast and coffee.'

'Aunt Benny. It's American comfort food. I would say it's good. You should come.'

We smile at each other. I don't think we are flirting.

'And what do you do in India?'

'I'm a psychotherapist.'

'Oh. I actually want to do an MA in psychology. I've applied at the university here.'

'Any particular field or topic that interests you?'

'Well, I'm interested in the dynamics of gay relationships. And I think it might be interesting to study here in Berlin. There is a certain freedom here. The other side of that can be a lack of commitment I think.'

'Have you dated here?' I ask.

'It's difficult,' Aron says.

'It's so difficult,' another guy says behind me. He seems a little drunk or high, but friendly, so Aron and I both smile at him. 'I've sort of done an experiment and tried to see how many of the guys I hook up with actually maintain eye-contact during sex,' he continues in a Russian-accented English, surprisingly articulate for his state. We look him in the eyes, though I am not sure how clearly he sees.

'And?' Aron asks.

'Almost none. They just look at my dick.' He looks down at his crotch ruefully. I immediately wonder how big it is. It is difficult to know whether we should laugh or remain serious. It is the way he says it. At the end of his sentence there was a sad sigh, I think. But it may also have been a chuckle. Even if it was, should we join in? Was it a pre-emptive laughter, him laughing at himself before others do? I smile instead. It is open enough to seem kind and understanding, I hope – a psycho-therapist smile, some might say. I think Aron chuckled but quickly stopped. All this in the blink of an eye.

'Hey.' David is back. He gives Aron a beer. 'You've made some more friends,' he says, looking at the other guy. 'I'm

David. Want some beer?'

'Thanks.' He accepts David's bottle and takes a gulp. 'I'm Ivan.' He hands the bottle back. We all say our names and shake hands.

'You have to also meet my friend here,' Ivan says and turns to a husky, East-Asian-looking guy standing next to him. 'Genghis,' Ivan continues. 'He is actually a descendant of Genghis Khan.'

Genghis smiles and shakes his head a little, saying, 'Well, a lot of us probably are. One in twelve in Asia, and one in 200 worldwide. He fucked around a lot, you know.'

We all introduce ourselves to Genghis.

There is finally some movement up ahead and hope spreads down the queue. We move one step, two, three, then stop again. We laugh resignedly. Ivan pulls out a bag of peanuts from his backpack, opens it and offers it to us.

'Bonding through trauma,' Aron says.

'Isn't this how all good relationships are built?' Ivan says. 'With commitment to a common goal, and sharing one's joys and suffering over time.'

My phone beeps with a message. It has been an hour and a half since the last one. 'Sorry the queue is so long. We could also take the party home to us.'

I wonder if they have slept at all since I met them last night. I never did go back to their place. I didn't have sex with anyone. Then, this morning, they texted me I should join them here. I reply, 'No worries. A community is forming here. Stories, food and drinks. I understand if you don't want to stay there forever though. Don't feel obliged to wait for me.'

I put away the phone, lean against the wall, look up at the sun and close my eyes, enjoying the sun on my face and listening to the voices and feeling the presence of the people around me. Ivan, Aron, David and Genghis are talking about life in Berlin. They talk of queuing and waiting. Ivan says that he waited for three hours at Accident and Emergency last week. 'The Accident and Emergency!' he says, shaking his head. He doesn't say what happened to take him there.

'I need to piss again. It's a thing when I drink,' David says. 'I'll get some more beer. Who wants?' Having taken people's orders, he is off again.

Ivan starts another story. I listen with only half an ear, but enjoy his voice and company.

Slowly, very slowly, we are moving towards the entrance of the club.

I check my phone. The couple have texted me to say that they will probably leave soon. 'I completely understand,' I text back. It is now 5.30 p.m. I look up and over at Aron. We both raise our eyebrows, sigh and smile.

After David has returned, more beer has been drunk and Ivan has told several more of his stories, we are even closer. The music is getting louder; disco and house. Sometimes Aron moves his shoulders and hips a little to the beat. I do too.

We can see the entrance clearly now. There is a conflict going on. A woman seems to have been refused entry and is insulting the bouncer loudly. I can understand her vexation, having waited so long. And bouncers in Berlin are notorious, I have gathered, for their arrogance and capriciousness. I look at my clothes – black shorts and a black T-shirt – and wonder if I will get in. I don't know what they are looking for here. I don't think it is a question of race; the queue and crowd seems to be quite mixed in that sense. The woman at the entrance is white, and it doesn't seem to be helping her. She leaves the queue, but then she runs up the side, along the barbed wire fence and past the trees, shouting that she is going to get in one way or another.

'I think we'll see her inside,' Ivan says. 'She has determination.'

I wonder how I would feel if I was refused entry. Embarrassed in front of all these people. Frustrated that I waited so long. But the queuing has been an experience in and of itself, I think to myself. That would be some consolation.

We are almost there now. The bouncer – shaven head, full beard, heavily tattooed – lets in one or two people ahead of us, waits for ten minutes or so, then lets in the next person. Slowly our community is dissolved.

'See you in there,' Aron says to me as he and David enter.

I am next. I wait for a long time – at least it feels like a long time – trying not to look directly at the bouncer, pretending to be reading something on my phone, not knowing what might provoke a negative reaction.

'Okay. You. 15 euros.'

I pay and enter.

Inside I at once feel high, a high from getting in, from getting in after waiting for so long, a high from the music and men and the ambience in here. The crowd is mixed but mostly made up of gay men. I need to take a piss and find the toilet. It's the grimmest I have ever seen, grimmer than toilets in India. Then I find a bar. There is a group of I think Brazilian men clustered there. One of them comes up to me, close, face to face.

'Hi,' he says. 'You are beautiful.'

He kisses me. I let it happen. Someone puts his hands on my hips. I turn. I kiss him as well. They are a group of friends on holiday. They share me willingly. I share of myself willingly. They invite me to join them on a large dancefloor. The room is booming with house beats and steaming with moving bodies, masculine sweat and scent. A pool of sensuality and excitement. We kiss and touch each other in between the dancing. But I just arrived and want to explore the place a bit more.

'I'm going to walk around a bit,' I say.

'Okay. We are here. Come back,' one of the Brazilians says.

I go to check out the outdoor area of the club. We are near a canal. Beyond it the sun is setting, lengthening our shadows. On the lawn stretching down to the water people are dancing. Others are sitting around a bonfire: the temperature is falling. After a stroll I go back inside to one of the bars, get some water and sit on a window sill, enjoying the refreshing breeze blowing through the open window and watching people.

'Hi.' A sexy guy comes close and positions himself between my legs, face to face, his hands on my thighs. He says his name. He is also Brazilian. Soon we kiss. He places my hand on his crotch. I wonder if he is part of the group I met earlier. Maybe we could all do a group thing. I have never done that and the idea intrigues me. I ask if he knows them. He doesn't.

Then I notice Aron.

'Aron.' I smile.

I introduce the two. Aron sits down next to me on the window sill.

'Your friends still here?' he asks.

'No,' I say. 'But that's okay.'

The Brazilian is now kissing a boy standing next to us.

Vikram Kolmannskog

'And David?'

'He found someone. They're busy getting to know each other.'

A guy comes up to Aron. 'Nice pecs,' he says. 'I like.' His hand flows over Aron's chest as he passes him.

I look at Aron's pecs. He does have a nice body. He notices me looking. I do it in an obvious, funny way, like I have just noticed. We could kiss and even have sex perhaps. We already have a certain intimacy. And I like him. But we won't. Not now. We just sit beside each other by the window and watch the room full of people and feel the breeze from the arriving night on our sweaty backs.

The Sacred Heart

I am walking. Alone. Ahead of me on the dirt road are an old man and woman. They have scallop shells on their rucksacks, signs that they too are on their way to Santiago de Compostela. They are walking slowly, leaning on their walking sticks and each other. I hoped we would become like that, an old couple like that. Couldn't we have tried harder? Couldn't we have tried a bit longer?

'Buen camino, young man,' the old man says, smiling, as I pass them.

'Buen camino,' I respond, and smile too.

I appreciate his greeting, bringing me back to awareness of what is here and now, wishing me well. And then me wishing them well in return. The greeting conveys a sense that we are on this journey together as well as separately. And his 'young man' reminds me that I am still young and hopefully have most of my life ahead of me.

Thor was my first love. I imagined that we would be together forever. When we broke up I was heartbroken and needed to get away and do something different. I was profoundly restless, and it was my mother who suggested I walk. I started today, a September afternoon, setting out from Saint Jean Pied de Port in France. Now I am crossing the Pyrenees into Spain. I walk for hours. White sheep dot the green hillside. An eagle soars above me, high up in the sky, the vast blue sky.

An ancient Roman road eventually takes me down through a forest of oaks and beeches, rustling leaves, swaying branches, into a valley. Just before dark I arrive at Roncesvalles, a medieval monastery. Here the monks offer travellers their hospitality as they have done for hundreds of years. I give them my name, Ram, a Hindu name. They don't ask about my religion or sexuality or anything else. It is enough that I am a pilgrim. They bless me. And offer me a bed and a thick wool blanket in the large dormitory hall.

The next day I set off shortly after dawn. I walk briskly in the cold morning. As the sun starts to warm me, I slow down and take off my jacket. A butterfly appears and accompanies me for a while. Then it flutters off to one side of the path, bringing my attention to a small cave in the hillside. I leave my rucksack outside and crawl in. It is dark. I sit down and close my eyes. I ask for a sign. I sit for a while, the air cool and slightly damp on my face. Opening my eyes again, I notice something red painted on the wall. The Sacred Heart. It is a sign that a great love exists, that hearts break and heal.

Rejoining the path and continuing on my way I notice more of these hearts and the words 'Dios es amor' painted on the surfaces of stones and buildings and road signs, or marked out with pebbles on the ground. 'God is love.'

The path cuts across a vineyard. Some pilgrims are taking a break here, just outside a monastery. From a tap on the wall flows free wine, courtesy of the monks. I join the group. We fill our water bottles with red wine, drink and talk. After a while I continue walking, a little tipsy under the bright, hot sun, and very touched by the generosity.

Further along, an old farmer picking apples in his orchard invites me in, offers me one. It is crisp and tart. I enjoy it. He insists on filling my rucksack with more. Again I am filled with gratitude. I overflow. As I continue walking, I meet another pilgrim and offer him one of the apples.

The pilgrims I meet come from all corners of the world, for a variety of reasons. Mostly I walk alone, at my own pace, exchanging no more than a 'buen camino' with others, the simple greeting enough to unite us. I follow the yellow arrows and scallop signs through open meadows and fields, fruit groves and forests, almost-abandoned villages and bustling cities, cold mist and hot sun. I sleep in basic refuges for pilgrims, hostels and, every now and then, fancier hotels. I get burning blisters on my feet. My shoulders become sore from the weight and chafing of my rucksack. I feel happier and happier.

Past the city of Pamplona I reach the Hill of Forgiveness. It is a steep climb. The top is decorated with a cast-iron sculpture of unspecified pilgrims on their way. I sit down in their cool shade. A light, swooshing sound comes from some white wind turbines catching the nearby breeze. I remember harsh words that I have said and things that I have done, to Thor and to others. Whispering I ask forgiveness from him and from others, from everyone and everything.

Late at night I reach a village at the foot of another mountain. Alone in a hostel room here, in the dark night, I again long for Thor. I forgive myself. And, as I fall asleep, I see his face. I kiss his lips softly. We are on the way somewhere and have stopped at a train station. He says something funny, and I laugh. I laugh so much that I wake myself up.

The following day I meet a man from Denmark on the road. He starts complaining about refugees. As we walk west towards the Atlantic Ocean, many refugees are arriving on Europe's southern coasts. There is much debate. I hope for dialogue. I listen to the man from Denmark. Then I talk about this walk, 'el camino'. Aren't we also migrants of one sort or another? Carrying only a rucksack and a walking stick, we are also at the mercy and the good will of others on this road. After a while I stop for a break and let him go on at his own pace. We say farewell with a 'buen camino.'

I reach the flat, yellow plateau of Castilla. The air is hot and dry. The sun burns my skin. For days I walk in almost complete silence. I practice listening, and start to hear more and more. When I come across some ancient-looking ruins late one evening, there is a gust of wind and I hear something resembling a scream. I decide to collect some pebbles and create a small heart here. Arriving in a nearby village, I enter a bar and ask about the ruins. The barman tells me they are the remnants of an old Jewish community abandoned during the Reconquista, when Jews and Muslims were persecuted and many fled the country.

When I arrive in the city of León there is a festival going on. I first stop in a small, quiet park on the outskirts. A statue of Saint Francis of Assisi stands there with open arms, smiling and praising all that lives. I close my eyes, smile and open my arms as well, sensing the air and sun and birds and trees. Later, as I enter the city, I hear another scream. As part of the festivities an eagle has been tied to a pillar in the middle of a plaza. For show. As a curiosity. The eagle cries pathetically, and my heart aches. But I don't know what to do. Quietly I ask its forgiveness and leave León.

After Castilla and León the green hills of Galicia, misty and cooler, are refreshing. I walk in rain and mist for a couple of days. And then, early one morning in an oak forest, I feel a sudden, warm touch on my back, and the mist lifts as if by magic. I turn and take in the first sunlight of the day. The warmth and light embrace the oaks around me as well. I look up at them. A dewdrop falls from one of the branches onto my forehead. It is cool. Like the monks at Roncesvalles – without asking about my religion or sexuality or anything else – the old oaks, mist and sunlight bless me.

After three weeks of walking I arrive in Santiago de Compostela. There I meet other pilgrims, including the Danish man who had complained about refugees, and we talk and eat and drink together. My mother flies in to meet me. We have a meal of local seafood, including scallops, and local Ribeiro wine. With her bad knees and strong will she joins me for the last stretch, to Finisterre, Land's End.

When we arrive on a hilltop from which we have our first view of the Atlantic Ocean, I suggest we create something together. We search for white pebbles on the path and in the surrounding meadow. Having collected several handfuls of these, we meticulously create a large, white heart, here on the hilltop. My mother and I are cheerful, like two children playing, and at the same time sincere and fully engaged in this task. Somehow she too seems to know that this is the most important thing in the world right now.

Having completed the heart, we continue walking, descending towards the glimmering ocean.

God is love.

When He Cut My Hair

I watch as he fills a brass lota with water, lifts it and pours it over his head.

The slow-flowing water of the river, ever new and fluid, meets the massive stone slabs that make up the ghat, ancient and immobile. And squatting there, on one of the lower steps nearest the river, is this beautiful man. He has a thin, white cotton towel wrapped around his waist, contrasting with his dark copper body. I watch how his back muscles work under the tight skin as he fills the lota, raises it and tips water over his head and down his body. Perhaps he is a pehlwan: he has a wrestler's build. Near him is a group of boys, younger, slimmer, but also fit. Perhaps all are pehlwans. One is squatting on the step above him, arms wrapped around his knees; another is standing, his feet set apart, his hands on his small hips. They also are looking at this man taking his morning bath.

He is beautiful, physically, but there is something more, another beauty added to that. It is in how he bathes. It is a ritual, starting with the head and then moving down the body. His every movement is so attentive: how he fills the lota, a respect for the lota, a respect for the water; how he pours it onto his body, a respect for the body; breathing; perhaps praying.

I remember how Papa used to wash the murtis in the temple. He would take each god and goddess, pour water over their bodies, then milk and honey, then rinse them with water again, and finally dry and dress them up for the day. He showed me how and let me help. I used to love taking part in that queer caring.

I look at the man again. He is standing now, facing the river. I see him from behind. I want to wash him, my hands on his body, respectfully. Would he let me though, an old man like me? He unwraps the towel and folds it. Underneath he is wearing a red langot, not covering much, generously revealing some of his round ass cheeks. My cock stirs and swells, a welcome sensation I have not had in a long time. I remember Abhishek. When his trousers came off and I discovered him wearing a thong that first time, the thin string, his marble ass, it made me crazy with lust. I pushed him onto the bed on his stomach, stroked his ass cheeks, lifted the string aside to reveal his rosy pink hole, rimmed him, smelling and tasting something reminiscent of the ocean, added some extra spit to his wet, soft hole, and then I fucked him, calling him bitch, calling him beloved.

I have seen images of Shiva wearing the langot. I know that our ancient scriptures associate it with asceticism and even celibacy. But with this skimpy piece of clothing, how can anyone think of celibacy? How can it not make men look and feel sexy? Shiva has always been my wild fantasy god. And his appearance, and the stories about him, have taught me that sexuality and spirituality go very well together. I mumble his name, a mantra, a mantra Papa first gave me.

The pehlwan is up to his waist in the river now, washing his jet-black hair, white lather making its way down his body to be carried away on the flowing water. I remember a story about Ganga that Papa must have told me; that she was a goddess whose powerful currents were tamed by being wound up in Shiva's locks. Shiva has thick, matted hair. Kali has unbound, unruly hair. Parvati has combed, well-bound hair. Krishna has curly hair. Abhishek had long and wavy hair, not unruly, not well-bound. His hair was golden brown. His eyes were amber. I remember first meeting him in his salon, feeling his delicate hands on my head and neck as he cut my hair; how much I wanted him as I watched him in the mirror.

I remember when Papa died, how Abhishek again cut my hair, but this time he cut it all off, a sacrifice of beauty, a surrendering of vanity and ego, first with scissors, then the single-blade razor. I remember the feeling of the blade, cold and hard, the pressure of his supple fingers, careful, silent. Less than a month later Ma also died. Abhishek stayed with me. He cared for me. When my hair grew back out, it was white. He said he liked it, the snow-white head hair and beard a contrast against my sandy brown skin.

I grieved a long time for my parents. Death in the abstract is one thing. You can philosophise. When it happens to you, when someone you love dies, it is something else. I let my hair and beard grow. Abhishek teased me, pulled my beard, called me Guru Dev. He asked to suck my cock and called me Daddy, but as soon as he had said it he realised his mistake and said sorry. He did his best. I did my best. But we grew more and more distant. Before we parted he cut my hair and beard one last time.

The pehlwan must have finished his morning bath. He is coming back out of the water now, facing the ghat, us, the langot cupping his cock and balls, nothing more, just the red langot, almost drawing more attention to that area than if he had worn nothing at all. He catches me looking at him; at least I think so: he looks at me directly. I look away. Shame floods me, an old man eyeing a young man like that. Maybe he is provoked, having seen the desire in my eyes. I remember how I used to react to old men: their attention felt somehow insulting to my youth and beauty, and I would get angry. But maybe it is different for him. Maybe he is flattered. Or maybe it doesn't even occur to him that there could be desire in me, this old man. If he comes up here after finishing his bath, if he passes nearby me, I will say something, tell him that he has a nice body perhaps. See what happens.

I am rather exhausted from all this excitement. I spread out my thick wool shawl and lie down, let my frail body be supported by the stone ghat. The spring morning sun is still soft.

I close my eyes for a moment.

When I wake up he is gone. So is the group of boys. I realise I have a hard-on and cover myself with the shawl. I remember dreaming that my cock was big like a lingam, boys and men lusting for it, someone pouring milk and water over it, over all of me, washing me. I dreamt something more, but I can't remember. Was it related to death and dying? Dreaming here by the river is like yoga, they say. Anyone who dies here is liberated, they say. Shiva whispers something in your ear; a reminder that we are already divine and free perhaps. I don't know, but I like the idea.

I decide to go for a haircut.

I make my way through the narrow alleys of old Varanasi and find a salon. Loud Hindi music and images come from a television on the wall. The barber is wearing a tight, pink T-shirt, tucked into tight trousers, his paunch pressing against the pink fabric. His mouth is full of paan, but he manages a few mumbled words as I sit down in the chair.

I look at myself in the mirror. Since Abhishek and I broke up fifteen years ago I have not cut my hair or beard. I have kept it neat and tidy though, my beard in a simple plait in the front, my hair similarly at the back. I don't know what I want. In the end I tell the barber to take everything.

As the scissors flash and I see the plait of white hair fall, I remember an article I read once about the big business of hair in India. Much of the hair exports, which total crores of dollars each year, come out of the tradition of offering hair at temples. It is collected up and made into wigs that are then sold abroad, mainly in Europe and North America. Most Indians who offer their hair in acts of religious devotion are unaware of this. And most of those who buy the wigs are equally unaware of the religious aspect involved. As his scissors clip close I wonder if this barber also collects and sells hair. I wonder if my hair will become part of a wig on the other side of the world. I look at it. It is not bad. It is something different, long and white. Whose wig might it become? I like the idea that various parts of me become part of something and someone else; that while I may disintegrate, life continues.

The barber has started shaving me now. I feel his grip firm on my skull. He gently pulls my head back, lets me rest it on his cushiony paunch. He puts a blade near my throat. This stranger, my life. I feel his finger near my lips. I close my eyes.

At some point we must be very close, his face and mine. I smell cardamom, clove, camphor and something else. I smell rose petals. I smell the sweetness from his mouth. I hear him breathing, close to my ear, in my ear, speaking.

Oh my god.

About the Author

Vikram Kolmannskog is a gay man of dual heritage, born to an Indian mother and a Norwegian father. He is based in Oslo, Norway, but considers both India and Norway his homes. He is the author of *Poetry Is Possible: Selected Poems*, *The Empty Chair: Tales from Gestalt Therapy*, and *Taste and See: A Queer Prayer*.

Photograph by Ahmed Umar

www.Vikram.no

Lightning Source UK Ltd.
Milton Keynes UK
UKHW010308180719
346343UK00001B/44/P